FIRE & ASH

SARA CATE

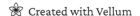

TRIGGER WARNING

Dear reader,

There is mention of child abuse, drug addiction, homophobia, and mental illness in this story. Please proceed with caution.

1

THOMAS

"You have to be fucking kidding me." There is steam billowing from the hood of my car, and lights are blinking at me from the dash as I fly down the freeway at eighty miles an hour.

Quickly, I pull my car off the road, stopping on the shoulder and jumping out before the damn thing explodes. This is what I get for being a stubborn asshole who refuses to buy a new car, even though this seventeen-year-old BMW has seen better days— much, much better days. If I call my best friend, Everly, right now and ask for help, she's definitely going to rub it in my face. She's been on me to replace this thing for years, but I'm being stubborn about it.

Fuck.

At least it's September, which means the temps have dropped and I don't risk dying of heat stroke out here. Standing a safe distance away, I pull out my phone and find the roadside assistance number.

Fifteen minutes later, the lovely girl on the line informs me that a mechanic in town will be here in less than an hour to tow me to their shop.

Halle-fucking-lujah.

This has really been the year from hell. Whoever said your thirties were supposed to be your best years was either delirious or high off their ass, because it would seem turning thirty-four last November set off a domino effect of bad luck.

In June, we lost our beloved editor-in-chief at the *Florence Journal* after he retired and moved to Florida, and instead of handing the job over to me—as it should have been, considering my twelve years of experience as a lead journalist, they gave it to that toolbag, Patrick from *The Herald*. They *outsourced* our new EIC when I am more than capable of taking on the position myself, and what's worse is that I'm about ninety percent sure, Patrick is a homophobe. More than once, he's denied my story requests because the articles would be better suited for—*quote-unquote*, someone with more guts.

So, I quit.

Excited for your first day tomorrow?

Everly texts me while I wait.

· · ·

I want to vomit every time I think about it.

That's normal, she replies with a laughing face emoji. *Couldn't be any worse than my first semester.*

God, I hope not. When Everly started her teaching job at Florence University, she had one of her biggest enemies as a student, who turned into her biggest tormenter, who then turned into the *'love of her life.'* Now they live together in some twisted domestic bliss, and I'm fairly certain they have some pretty kinky shit going on in the bedroom, so I'd say it turned out all right.

For her, at least. Settling down, with a college student no less, sounds more like a nightmare than all the bullying he did to her in those first few months, but that's just me.

I don't have any mortal enemies from my past, so I think I'm golden.

Just be your charming, brilliant, funny self, and they will love you.

. . .

Why the fuck is my best friend so amazing to me? Where did I go right twelve years ago when we met, because I could use a little good luck like that in my life right now.

Thanks, babe. That helps. Love you.

Love you too. Seriously, Thomas. Don't be nervous. You will be great.

Just don't fuck your students. I know how young you like them.

Bitch. You have absolutely no room to talk.

While I'm smiling down at my phone, I hear the rumble of a truck approach. Damn, that was fast. I'm leaning against the car, pretty convinced it's not going to blow up since the smoking has stopped, when the driver of the tow truck jumps out, and I'm struck speechless.

I was expecting a typical mechanic—middle-aged and greasy. Not a Greek God in blue coveralls.

He's damn near the tallest man I've ever seen in my life. With broad shoulders and thick biceps, I can't seem to tear my eyes away as he stalks closer. When I do force my gaze to his face, the first thing I notice are the scars etched into his features. It looks like someone took a box-cutter to what must have been a flawless facade with those high cheekbones, a sharp jawline, a chiseled nose...

"Mr. Litchfield?" he says in a rich, deep voice. Jumping up from my position against the car, I take a couple steps toward him.

"That's me."

"I got a call that you need a tow to the shop. What seems to be the problem?"

"Well, a lot of smoke came out of the hood, which I'm assuming is bad, so I pulled over right away."

"Can I take a look?" he asks as he passes by me, leaving behind a cloud of his masculine scent.

Upon closer inspection, I realize he's young, or at least younger than I thought at first—maybe early twenties? I also notice his lips are full and perfect. There's a slash through the top one, and I instantly find myself wondering what it might feel like against my tongue.

"Sir?"

"Oh, yeah. Go ahead." I hold a hand up, gesturing to the front of my car.

He hesitates, glaring at me with his brows pinched together. "I need you to open the hood for me," he says in a bold command that sends a flash of heat all the way down my spine.

"Umm..." I open the driver's side door and crouch down in search of the lever to unlock the hood. I fumble around for a few seconds but can't seem to find it.

"You don't know where the hood latch is, do you?" I feel his presence behind me, and a wave of frustration rolls through me. I'm having a bad enough day/month, and I don't need to be humiliated by a kid with a tow truck.

"I just forgot where it is," I mutter. Pulling a handle, I hear a pop and stand up, relief consuming me. As he pins me between his body and my car, he looks down at me with a look of amusement on his face, and I notice that I barely come up to his chin.

"That was your gas tank."

Dick.

Kneeling down again, I fumble for the handle, my temperature rising and making it difficult to focus. I freeze when I feel his arm brush mine. He's towering over me from behind, and I breathe in the scent of cologne mixed with oil and gasoline. One of his hands lands on my arm as he crowds me, and though there is grease between his nails and caked into the prints of his fingers, I notice that it's softer than I expected. It takes him exactly one second to find the lever under the dash, which results in a popping noise from the front of the car.

In my defense, I'm more of a 'drop it off at the mechanic and let them deal with it' kind of guy.

"Thanks," I mumble as he walks away.

He inspects the car's engine, pulling out and opening up parts I have absolutely no knowledge about, and I can't seem to shake this sudden unnerved spell he's put me under. How have I never seen him around town? Surely I'd remember a guy like him. He must be at least six-four, maybe five, and those *scars*. His chin-length black hair hangs in his face as he messes around underneath the hood, and I try my damndest to look interested in what he's doing, but I can't imagine it's very convincing.

"Try to start it for me." Again with that commanding tone.

I drop into the driver's seat and turn the ignition. The car sounds like it wants to start, but all it does is pop and rev without moving into a steady rhythm.

"Cut it!" he yells over the noise. Doing as he says, I take the key out and climb back out of the seat, just as he flips his hair out of his face.

Okay, that was hot.

"Looks like your radiator," he says while inspecting the engine.

"Okay." As if I have any clue what the fuck that means.

"I can tow it to the shop for you. I don't think I have the parts, but I could have it done in a couple days."

"That would be great, thanks." I keep staring at his face, no matter how hard I try not to. I mean, it's pretty damn hard not to. Those scars are not like any I've seen before, and the reporter in me wants the story—the *whole* story. It literally looks like someone carved into this poor kid's face. And they've faded to a light hue which means they're old, probably something he got as a little kid.

"You can ride to the shop with me, unless you have someone coming for you..."

"No one is coming for me," I blurt out so fast I surprise myself. What the fuck was that all about? It's like I was trying to announce that I'm single, as if he fucking cares. That's clearly not what he was asking. *He's not hitting on you, you fucking pervert.*

He slams the hood shut, and I notice the way his gaze lingers on me for just a second, and it's enough to send chills down my spine.

When he goes back to his truck, he throws it into reverse and lines it up with mine. I watch in some sort of erotic fascination as he hoists the chain out of the truck, setting everything up on my car and effortlessly chaining it to the rear of the truck.

Did he just make loading a tow truck sexy?

If I were in the middle of a dry spell, I'd assume this strange interest was due to needing to get laid, but I got lucky, not once, but twice this weekend. In fact, that's where I was headed home from, a sleep-over at my FWB's—*friend with benefits.* Nico and I have been carrying on a no-strings-attached hookup for a couple years now. It's completely casual and not at all *coupley.* He's pushing his late twenties, and I keep waiting for him to give me the nudge that he's ready to settle down, but it hasn't really happened yet, and honestly, I don't know how I'll feel when it does. I like Nico, and we have a good time together, but the idea of forever with him doesn't exactly get me *excited*.

"Ready to go," Mr. Tall Tow Truck Man barks, jerking his head toward the cab of the truck and signaling for me to get in. As I step up into the seat, the first thing I notice is just how much it smells like him, a combination of cologne and grease with a hint of mint and air freshener. I don't know why, but it reminds me of my teenage years, and I'm hit with a wave of nostalgia, inciting a wave of memories of making out with various boys in cars that smelled like this. I'm pretty sure I gave my first hand job in a truck like this. Back then, I was so sexually pent-up and frustrated, desperate to get it out, I let any guy who wanted to touch me have his way. They were good fucking times.

The mechanic is staring at me with a quizzical brow, and I glance his way after buckling my seatbelt.

"What is it?" I ask.

"You're the one who looks like you want to say something."

"No, I don't," I argue.

He laughs. "Yes, you do. You're judging my truck. I'm sorry it's not as nice as your early 2000's BMW."

"I was not judging your truck," I snap. "I was just remembering something..."

He laughs again. "You have some fond memories in tow trucks, Mr. Litchfield?"

"That's a forward question."

"Sorry," he mutters as he puts the truck into drive.

We turn onto the freeway, merging with traffic, and I notice immediately how eerily quiet it is in the car now. He was being casual with me, which was unexpected, and I reacted too harshly. So now it's awkward, and I regret it. The kid was just being friendly. It's not his fault I'm off today, in a bad mood and a serious funk.

"Not in *tow trucks* specifically," I add, desperate to break the tension. Then, my blabber mouth just keeps rambling. "But something about this one brought back memories of high school. I must have dated someone with a truck that smelled like this."

The words slip out before I can really think about what I'm admitting.

Why did I say that? Why the fuck did I say that?

I wince, knowing that I just made things even more awkward as I'm sure he's putting two and two together now. *Girls* don't normally drive trucks like these.

"Good memories, I assume?" he asks with his eyes on the road.

When I glance over at him, I notice how tightly he's gripping the steering wheel and clenching his jaw, clearly indicating his discomfort. *God, let this ride end quickly.*

"Yeah, sure. They were good memories," I mumble.

He turns to look at me. "What? You don't remember?"

"It was a long time ago," I reply.

There is a subtle smile as he looks at me again.

Then his eyes travel from my face and down my body, as if he's sizing me up. I feel the hot sting of his judgment, and I swear I am all too tempted to dive out the window of this moving vehicle and into freeway traffic.

"How long ago?" There's no longer a cruel look on his face; now it almost seems...flirtatious, and I notice that he has warm amber-colored eyes that look like the cat-eye rocks I used to collect as a kid. The irises shine in different shades of brown and red like a burning fire.

"Well, let's see. I was a teenager..." I do the match quickly in my head, "fifteen years ago."

His eyebrows shoot up. "That *was* a long time ago."

"Oh, fuck you very much," I reply, and his laughter fills the truck. My nerves dissipate as I realize he's being genuine, not a homophobic asshole like I feared, and his teasing me about my age is almost coming across as...sexy, somehow.

"Sorry," he says, still laughing, and I can't help but smile. "It's only been one year for me."

"One year since you were a teenager?" I ask, rolling my eyes. "Enjoy your youth while it lasts. Blink and you'll miss it."

He nods his head, seemingly contemplative. Then there's another few minutes of silence, which he breaks when he asks, "So, you haven't been in a truck since you were a teenager?"

"Um...not really. I'm not much of a truck guy."

"Obviously," he replies.

"What's that supposed to mean?"

"You didn't even know how to pop the hood of your car. I assume you've never driven a truck."

"I could drive a truck," I toss back.

"I believe you." When he looks at me, his grin is so deep in his cheeks that it creates dimples around the scars. I find myself staring at them, fascinated by how they stretch across his face, and my fingers itch to trace the lines of each one.

I feel strangely comfortable around this guy now. I like his flirty banter, although I know I have no right to because he's not flirting. Even if he was gay—which I guarantee he's not, he's not my type.

I don't really do the slum-down thing. My type is more like Nico, fit, young, and *flexible*. Slightly submissive and easy to manipulate—in bed and in our relationship.

We turn into the parking lot of the mechanic shop and pull right into the first bay. I'm surprised to see it quiet and empty. He puts the truck into park, and I expect him to jump out, but he pauses in his seat. The moment stretches as he stares out the window. "For what it's worth," he says, finally. "You don't look thirty-four."

"Thanks," I reply quietly.

His head turns my way, and our eyes lock. I'm lost in those amber brown irises for a moment, waiting for him to say or do something to break the sudden tension. But he doesn't. Instead, we bathe in the uncertainty between us because there's something about it—or *him*, that feels both hot and cold, ice and fire in my veins. But it's the fire and strange anticipation that makes its way down to my groin.

He finally jumps out of the vehicle, and I take my first full breath in minutes.

I sit in the truck for a moment, letting this strange feeling wash over me, willing the sudden arousal in my pants to chill the fuck out.

When I finally hop out, he's already unloading my car off the back of the truck, so I busy myself with walking around and looking at everything. It's not a big shop, and it's isolated on a road just outside of the city center. It's in good condition though, cleaner and newer than I thought it would be.

"You run this place by yourself?" I ask.

He laughs. "No. I'm just the only guy willing to work on Sundays."

"What's wrong? You don't go to church?"

That dimpling grin stretches on his face again, revealing perfectly white teeth. As he looks up at me, he replies with a small shake of his head, "No, I don't."

I watch him maneuver the car until it's parked in the bay and hoisted six-feet in the air, and I realize that I could easily watch this guy at his job all day long. It's like foreplay—this sensual dance of muscles and effort and sweat, those strong yet nimble hands moving with deft skill and experience, imagining them working the same way on my clothes and my body.

He catches me looking a few times, but I play it off

as just interest in what he's doing, and he seems mostly unfazed.

"If you'd like to meet me in the office," he says casually, "we can fill out some paperwork before you leave."

Is that his not-so-subtle way of trying to get rid of me? Giving him a nod, I head in the direction of the entrance. Going through the black door on the side of the garage, I find a small office, immaculately clean, with a broad wooden desk, a computer, and a couple chairs for customers. But I don't sit down. I'm feeling too restless. I'd rather just settle this now, call my Uber, and put this shit show of a day and very strange encounter behind me.

Just as I pull up the Uber app on my phone, I hear him coming in. With my back to the door, I hear the distinct sound of the door closing and the lock clicking. Everything in me freezes, and my head gets caught in a vicious battle between fear and anticipation. This could either be a very good thing or a very bad thing.

The space is swallowed up in silence as he takes another heavy step closer to where I'm standing. My heart seems to be the only thing in the room moving as I wait for what comes next. I'm either about to be fucked or murdered, and my body is wound so tight in arousal and anticipation it doesn't seem to know the difference.

I don't know why, but I expect him to say something, to flirt with me some more or ask me out, but he doesn't. Instead, he pounces.

His large hand takes me by the throat, pulling me backward until I'm up against the hard wall of his body. Then soft lips are devouring my neck, and what comes out of my mouth barely sounds human.

I'm fifty-percent turned on and fifty-percent glad to be alive.

Okay, maybe ninety-ten.

His groan is loud in my ear, and his kiss is ravenous, warm lips and tongue sucking eagerly on my jaw and then my earlobe. I'm thrust into the sensation of complete euphoria.

One hand is still on my neck, holding me in a punishing grip so I can't move—not that I'd want to, while the other is traveling down my side until he reaches around to the front of my body and cups my quickly growing erection through my pants. Then, he grinds himself against me, squeezing me tight in his hands. The hard length of his cock is crushed against my lower back.

I'm five-eleven. Almost tall, and definitely not short. In this guy's arms, though, I might as well be four feet tall by the way he's handling me, and I don't hate it. Right now, I don't hate anything because I'm being groped by a perfect stranger, not even old enough to drink alcohol, in the office of a mechanic's shop. On a fucking Sunday.

"Fuck," I groan out when he strokes his hand down my dick with perfect precision. *Please fucking take it out,* I pray. And like a sign from God himself, my handsy mechanic fumbles with the buttons on my jeans. They're unzipped in seconds, and his hungry hand digs into my boxers for my aching cock.

Once he has his giant fingers around me, I thrust forward. He strokes me hard to the rhythm of his grinding against my backside. His lips keep up their assault on my neck, and my hands don't quite know what to do. I reach back with one hand and grab onto his hip, pulling him harder against me, while the other one slides up his arm until I reach his head, skating through his soft hair and tugging his face closer.

"Take your fucking pants off," he bites out in a sexy command.

I tense for only a moment. It's not that I have a problem bottoming—it's just that I'm not usually so eager to do so. But apparently, when this guy says jump, I say fuck me.

Digging my thumbs into my waistband, I shove my pants down fast, taking my boxers with them. He lets go of my cock and fumbles in his back pocket, and I hear the familiar crinkle of a condom wrapper. When I glance back, he has it pinched between his teeth along with a packet of lube.

Our eyes meet for a heated moment, but he quickly averts his gaze, looking down as he opens his coveralls. Desperate for a look at his body, my eyes follow the zipper, but they don't get very far. His hand grasps hard at my face, turning me forward, so I can't see him.

"Put your hands on the fucking desk."

Obediently, I slide my palms along the cool

surface, my body frozen in anticipation, and my mind lost in a fog of confusion and arousal. It can't seem to keep up with this sudden whirlwind of events, and I don't really care. I don't need my mind to try and rationalize my decisions right now.

Suddenly, his hands are on my ass, spreading my cheeks, and he actually fucking *growls* in approval.

Am I dead? Did I fucking die and this is what my brain has conjured up as heaven? Fucking pinch me.

Something slick and warm slides along the cleft of my ass, and I shudder when his thick fingers, stretch me one by one. I'm moaning and writhing impatiently while he preps me, too eager to have him fuck me, but enjoying the process.

After slipping his fingers out, in a flash, the head of his cock prods my entrance. Pressing my hips back, I practically impale myself, and it occurs to me as he breaches the tight ring of muscle that I don't even know his name. But I let him in anyway. My body opens for him like he commanded it to do.

He lets out a hearty groan as he slides in another inch, and I'd be groaning along with him if I could breathe—but the sensation is too intense. It burns, but the pain lies because all I feel is pleasure.

He holds onto my hips as he fucks me deeper another few inches. When he rubs against my prostate, my knees practically turn to jello. With torturous control, he retreats and leisurely slides in again. It's a slow torment—I wish he'd just let himself go.

"Fuck me," I say through gritted teeth.

His movements pick up speed, causing my hands to keep losing their grip on the desk as he pounds into my body. I've never loved the feeling of being used and so selfishly fucked before, but the idea of being this twenty-year old's fuck toy has some strange appeal to it. With all those fucking scars and those bright eyes and wicked smile, I get off on the idea that my body could bring him pleasure, and I want him to take it.

His hand is back around my throat, and I'm pulled upright until I'm pressed against his chest. His mouth is next to my ear.

"You feel so good around my cock."

I groan again, his filthy words sending shockwaves coursing through my body. He reaches around for my dick, moving in rhythm with his thrusts and squeezing the head on every upstroke. The fronts of my thighs are digging into the desk, but I don't fucking care, because he's right; I do feel good around his cock, and his tight grip on my dick is making it hard to think straight.

"I'm gonna come," I moan.

"Paint my desk with it," he replies, and with a couple harsh slams of his body in mine, I'm done. The climax nearly knocks me off my feet, stealing the air from my lungs as wave after wave of pleasure courses through my veins. I don't just spill cum all over the surface of his desk—I'm pretty sure I saw some reach the floor on the other side. A moment later, his thrusting slows and I feel him shiver out his orgasm, a loud gasping groan echoing against the four walls. My neck is still locked in the vise grip of his large hand, my pulse pounding against his fingers. I'm almost afraid I won't be able to stand on my own when he lets go.

"Jesus," I gasp as my body recovers, my heart rate slowing and my lungs finally taking in a full breath of air.

He pulls out and quickly turns around, leaving me exposed. My muscles ache as I lean down to reach my pants around my ankles to pull them up. I hear him remove the condom, tossing it into the trash by the door. When I glance back again to see his face, he's already zipped up his coveralls and is avoiding my gaze.

Neither of us say anything. I mean, this isn't my first stranger quickie, but I have a feeling it might be his.

"So did you need me to fill out some paperwork or..."

"No," he grits out, "I have your number. I'll call you when your car is ready."

And just like that, he walks out of the office. I can barely move for a few moments, but when I finally regain the ability to think and breathe and function, I pull out my phone and order the Uber, hoping they'll arrive quickly to avoid any further awkward interaction. Then, I take a minute to clean up my mess before I exit the office.

Just as I cross the garage, my ride pulls up, and I glance toward the mechanic one last time before disappearing into the car. Too bad he doesn't even bother to look up at me as I leave.

While I'm in the car on the way to my house, I pull up my text conversation with Everly.

Well, I had an interesting morning...

2

PAX

My phone alarm blares from the floor, and I reach over to grab it and hit snooze. It's too early, too *fucking* early. Why do I sign up for 8:00 a.m. classes? What the fuck is wrong with me?

Oh yeah, because I have to squeeze in school around work. And rugby.

Sitting up on the thin foam mattress, I rub the sleep out of my eyes and try to muster enough energy to get up. There's not enough padding to keep me from feeling the cold concrete of the garage floor, but it's better than trying to get a good night's sleep in my car.

Glancing around the dim room, I see the office door and it sparks a memory from yesterday like an assault on my mind. As if I could forget fucking a complete stranger in my boss's office.

Why am I suddenly faced with a sense of nagging guilt? He was clearly into me; he never said no, and it was completely consensual. So we fucked. So what?

Because he's a *guy*.

Not the first guy I've fucked—not even close. Just the first one in broad daylight, at work, and who had seen my face beforehand. Dark encounters are really more my style. There's more anonymity and privacy in the darkness. But I couldn't help myself. That salty, short beard of his along with his tight ass caught me off guard.

I wish I could say I'd never see him again, but I have to fix his car and the parts are coming in tomorrow, so... looks like I will have to face him again. *Fantastic.*

I brush my teeth in the bathroom sink, shove my flimsy mattress in the storage closet no one opens, and toss a granola bar in my pocket as I run out the door. As I jump into my black and silver 1970 Chevelle SS, I say a little prayer that she starts for me on the first try, and thank fuck, she purrs to life after only a few seconds.

"Good girl, Aphrodite," I say, patting the steering wheel.

She may not have a working radio or A/C, and the heater may smell like something died in there, but she's mine. I bought her off an old lady whose husband had just died and she cared more about getting rid of it than getting rich off of it, so I put a whole month's salary toward the purchase. And three months' rent—hence the current living situation.

I was prepared to be homeless for Aphrodite.

When you live your entire life bouncing around foster homes, living in your car doesn't sound like such a sacrifice. For once in my life, I have something I own, something that's *mine*.

As I pull up to campus, I don't even bother looking at my schedule again. This is my second year at Florence U, and I'm here for two reasons.

One, rugby. When a disfigured orphan finds something he's good at, and it makes people revere him as a god, he doesn't let it go so easily.

Two, the grants from the state don't cover tech schools. And if I ever want to run my own shop someday, I need an education.

My academic advisor filled my schedule with all the shit I need, and I have to keep a passing grade. So far, it hasn't been an issue. I work, I play, I do my school work. That's it.

And occasionally, fuck strangers on a whim, apparently.

I still can't get that guy out of my head.

Thomas Litchfield. I didn't even know I was into older guys until now, but he was sexy as fuck. The way he groaned when I slid my cock into him, his fingers gripping the desk. The way he nearly shot his load three feet when he came. How good he tasted when I kissed his neck, like sweat and spice.

Fuck, it's only seven-thirty in the morning and I'm about to get out of my car with a chub in my pants. I have a few minutes to spare, so I do my best to *not* think about my cock in his ass and pray my dick deflates.

I catch a glimpse of myself in the rearview mirror.

He wasn't repulsed by me. It's not that he didn't stare—everyone does, but he didn't gape at me in disgust or confusion like people usually do. He had a keen interest in me, judging by the way his eyes lingered on my lips and eyes, almost like he was attracted to me. Maybe that's why I pounced on him in the office. I don't get that look a lot.

Grotesque repulsion? Absolutely. Fear and paranoia? Definitely. Curiosity? Sure.

But attraction? Nope. Never.

I'm used to it though. The guys on the team crack jokes, and I don't mind. I let it roll off my shoulders, and I laugh along when they call me Leatherface and the *ugly fuck*. Because we all know what really matters —I'm the best fucking player on the team. So they can have their fun giving me names. I just pound them into the pitch during practice.

Five minutes to eight, my dick has finally gotten the memo that now is not the time to get excited, so I jump out of the car and head into the English building. My first class is in the big lecture hall, and when I get there, it's already crammed with students. There's only a couple spots left, but they both require me to walk past the whole crowd, something that immediately has me clenching up with paranoia.

Pulling my hoodie over my head, I keep my eyes forward as I make my way across.

Then I hear a familiar voice.

"Come get a syllabus before you sit down," he says, his voice loud enough not to need the microphone that some teachers use. I freeze in my spot before glancing in his direction, and there he is.

Warm gray-speckled brown beard, tall narrow frame, long fingers, and tight slacks snug around his hips. When our eyes meet, time stops. Everyone in the room ceases to exist.

The man I fucked yesterday is my new English professor.

Of fucking course he is.

Someone behind me grabs my attention by shouting my last name across the room. "Hey, Smith! Get your shit and come sit down."

I glance back toward the voice and see one of my teammates, Mason Richards, hollering at me. There's an empty seat next to him, so I toss him a quick wave before jogging down to the front to grab the packet from the professor without looking him in the eye. Then I hightail my ass up to the third row to sink into a seat next to my friend.

"Too early for you or something?" he asks.

"Way too fucking early," I reply.

I have to keep my head down to keep from glancing back at Thomas. What if he says something or flirts with me? My skin is crawling, and I'm tempted to just bolt now. I can go straight to my advisor's office and change my schedule. It's not too late.

"Stay out too late?" Mason asks.

"Nah. Just worked all weekend."

"That sucks."

I sneak a glance up at Thomas, and he looks nervous, maybe a bit more now that he knows I'm here. How the fuck did I not notice he was a teacher here? My dumb ass had to go and fuck a professor without even knowing it.

Pulling my hood farther over my head, I sink into my chair while Thomas goes through the syllabus. I feel eyes on me, and I glance to the side to see a girl at the end of the row in front of us staring at me. I press my lips together and nod in her direction. Mason knocks me on the arm and lifts his eyebrows suggestively.

He thinks she's flirting with me.

He's an idiot because he doesn't realize a few very crucial things.

First of all, she's not flirting. Girls don't flirt with me. They stare because they're curious, and in her mind, I'm sure she's envisioning herself with me and wondering what it might be like.

Secondly, neither Mason nor any of the guys on my team know that I'm gay. It's bad enough being this ugly. I don't need to be given shit for anything else. Not that I think the guys on my team would call me a faggot for liking dick. It's more that I'm afraid they'll just treat me differently. Like they'll actually *stop* calling me ugly and Leatherface and worry about hurting my feelings. I'd much rather have guys who can crack jokes with me and treat me like any other player on the team.

I make it through the whole class without incident. Thomas does a decent job of focusing on teaching and I focus on taking notes and being a regular student. After class, Mason lingers a little too long and he gets stuck talking to one of the girls behind him.

I tap him on the shoulder, say a quick goodbye and dart out of the lecture hall. Thomas doesn't stop me. He does watch me go though, and it's so fucking awkward, I hate it.

I only have one more class today. Then I work at the garage for a couple hours before rugby practice at five. My packed schedule leaves me barely enough time for lunch, so I grab something fried and greasy on my way to work. When I get there, I find the parts for Thomas's car locked up in the back.

"Fuck," I curse out loud. I'm not an actual mechanic, so while I can do things like oil changes and tire rotations, full radiator repairs have to be done by a couple of the senior guys. So when I find them working away tirelessly on his car, I know it won't be long before I have to call him to pick it up.

"Hey," I say to Ivan as I cross the bay heading toward the office where I can sit down and eat my lunch.

"Hey, Pax," he replies. "I'll be done with this car today. You wanna call the customer and let him know?"

"Umm...can you call him? I have practice at five." My cheeks burn and my blood turns to ice as Ivan glares at me like I just kicked his dog.

"Calling the customers is your fucking job, man. Are you saying you can't do your job now?"

Fuck. "No. I can do it," I reply, stalking grumpily toward the office. His invoice is waiting for me, and I stare down at his name that I scribbled there yesterday. What a fucking idiot I was to even lay a hand on a customer. I'm lucky I didn't lose my job. It's not the first time I've been thankful the cameras don't work in the shop. There's no going back now.

Picking up the office phone, I quickly dial the number listed on the yellow paper. He answers on the third ring.

"Hello?"

"Mr. Litchfield..." I say, making my voice a touch deeper than it usually is. "This is Pax with Olympus Auto Shop. Your car is ready."

"Oh, Pax," he replies as if he's just realizing who I am. We never did properly exchange names yesterday. "Will you be around this evening? I can come by to get it."

"I have practice until seven."

"After seven works."

I wince.

"Perfect, then I'll...see you tonight."

"Thanks, Pax," he replies, saying my name again.

After hanging up, I rub my temple. It was supposed to be a quick hookup without attachments or feelings or names, but now I'm getting caught up on how good he looked at the front of the class today and how my name sounds rolling off his tongue. When he picks up his car, I'll keep my cool, act like nothing happened, and make it through the rest of the semester that way too.

How hard could it be?

3
THOMAS

"You didn't." Everly gasps across the table from me.

I laugh around my bite of fettuccini. "I wish."

"It's only the first day! I strictly said no sleeping with the students."

"Yeah well, when *he* was fucking *me,* he was only my mechanic."

"Oh, let's come back to that," she replies, noting how I mentioned the 'fucking me' part of that sentence. I really do tell Everly everything. "But what are you going to do now?"

"Sweetheart, there's more."

Her eyes widen, waiting for me to finish my sentence. "When I asked if I could pick up my car tonight, he informed me he has practice on campus until seven."

She drops her fork and grabs my arm. "He's on the rugby team."

"Yep."

"With Cullen."

"Yep."

"Oh that is hella complicated, Thomas," she replies. "Who is it?"

I can't help but wince, because there is a zero percent chance she doesn't know exactly who it is. Cullen, Everly's boyfriend, is now a senior at Florence U, and has been a star on the team for the past four years. He took a one-year hiatus after getting shot a few years back, but he's been back at it since the start of his junior year. She is a devoted girlfriend and goes to every game and as many practices as she can.

As for the public status of their student-teacher relationship, the administration was apparently so desperate for journalism professors, they basically told them not to let anyone see them together, and they'd let their relationship slide without Ev losing her job.

"More importantly," I say, "do you know of any openly gay players on the team?"

She wrinkles her nose. "No, but it's not exactly my business. Or anyone's for that matter."

"I'm willing to bet this year's salary that he's in the closet."

"Okay, but seriously. Who is it?"

"Pax?" I mutter quietly, remembering him on the phone, hearing him say his name for the first time. It all feels like such a mistake—the hookup, the being in my class, all of it. He never wanted me to know his name at all, but now I'm talking about his sexuality to a girlfriend of one of his teammates, which feels completely intrusive.

"Pax Smith?!"

"Shhh! Will you keep your voice down?" We're sitting in the campus cafe, and although we're far enough away from anyone hearing us, I still don't need to draw any more attention to Pax or this conversation.

"The tall kid with the..." Her voice trails as she gestures to her face.

"Yes, the six-foot-five Greek God with the facial scars."

She lets her gaze settle on me for a moment. "Really?"

He's not my type *at all*, which is exactly what she's thinking at this very moment. Other than the fact that he's much younger than me, there is nothing about Pax that would have led to me trying to get into his pants before he forcibly found his way into mine.

"Don't say it," I snap, before tossing my napkin on my plate and looking at my watch. "We better get going. It's almost seven."

Everly and I walk together across campus and head toward where the rugby players are finishing up practice. I keep my distance, not wanting Pax to see me with Everly or Cullen. It's bad enough I've shown up at his school and in his class; he doesn't need me popping up at his games and hanging out with one of his senior teammates.

It would seem that if avoiding being seen by

someone was a skill, I would be terrible at it, because as I cross between the cars in the parking lot and head toward Everly's car, I nearly slam right into all six and half feet of muscled, Adonis-body, Pax Smith.

"Shit," I mutter, clutching my chest. "You scared me."

Before I have a moment to collect myself, I'm being slammed against the backside of a van. But not the good kind of slammed. When I look up at Pax, he's snarling at me.

"What are you doing here?" He growls through clenched teeth. His hair is wet, hanging in his face, and he smells like Irish Spring soap. Even being fucked by him I wasn't close enough to him to really see him like this.

"I'm walking to my friend's car," I reply, pointing toward Everly's SUV. He turns and glances at the car, letting out a heavy exhale as if he's putting it all together now. "Until I get my car back, looks like I have to catch a ride everywhere." I try to sound casual, but it's a weak attempt.

When his gaze lands back on my face, he looks as if he's trying to maintain his composure. His hand is no longer on my chest, but he's still crowding me, only inches away, and I can tell it's an intimidation tactic, as if he needs one.

"Did you know last night that I was a student here? That I would be in your class?"

I flinch. "What? No! How would I know that?"

Voices carry across the lot, and we realize that Cullen and Everly are heading this way.

"Did you?" I ask.

He looks shocked, his teeth clenched and his nostrils flaring. "Of course not." He glances up, hearing the happy couple only a few cars away. Pax then leans in toward me again, and I breathe in his clean scent, my senses feasting on his nearness, even while he basically threatens my life. "Don't tell a fucking soul about yesterday, understand? I don't know you and you don't know me. You even think about telling anyone and I'll—"

"Pax, I won't," I whisper.

"Oh, there you are," Everly says, approaching me from behind. Pax leaps away from me, and when Ev's gaze lands on his face, she does a very poor job of hiding what she knows. "Oh, hi. Hello. Hey, Pax."

I wince. *Real smooth, Ev.*

Quickly, I try to salvage the situation. "Pax is my mechanic," I blurt out, and she tries to look surprised, but it's awful. This whole situation is awful.

Now Pax basically knows that I've told Everly about us, which is exactly what he just threatened me *not* to do.

Even though I wasn't in the closet for very long, I remember the agony of feeling like the most vulnerable, most private part of myself was at risk of becoming everybody else's business; it was terrifying. People are cruel, and they don't have compassion when it's not their own heart they're ripping to shreds.

Footsteps approach again, and I freeze when I see Cullen's short black hair come into view. He slaps Everly on the ass. "Let's go. I'm fucking starving."

His eyes land on me and Pax, who is suddenly sucked into this whole situation, standing with the three of us and looking like he wants to evaporate into dust.

"Hey, Smith," Cullen says, greeting his teammate.

Pax replies with a curt nod. I notice the way he keeps his head tilted away from people, sometimes facing down, and when given the chance, he seems to blend into his surroundings rather than try to stand out. It pulls at my heart a little, to see him try to hide himself. And try as I might not to stare, I sort of love his scars.

"Car, now," Cullen tells Everly, "I'm starved." It's taken some getting used to hearing the way he talks to her, and at first, I'll admit, I hated it. But I've never seen a guy so enamored by a woman fourteen years older than him. Plus, I think in some weird way, she likes his crass attitude and bossy ways.

"We have to drop Thomas off at the shop," she replies, calling after him. Anxiety settles in my bones when I realize what is about to happen.

"His shop?" Cullen replies, pointing to Pax. "Why doesn't Pax just take him. He's got a better car, anyway."

"You don't have to drive me," I say immediately,

trying to break the tension before it even builds. *Dammit, Cullen.*

Pax looks tense, his jaw is clenched and he's fisting his bag in one hand so tightly that his knuckles are white. I want to tell him to relax, that no one will suspect he's gay just because he gives me a ride to his shop. Then again, maybe he's tense because he doesn't want to be alone with me again. Maybe he hated every minute of it, and is actually repulsed by me.

Okay that's a dramatic assumption.

"It's fine. Makes more sense anyway," he says with a shrug of his shoulders.

"Are you sure?" I ask.

"Yeah, it's fine. Come on."

I wave goodbye to Everly and she grimaces at me before mouthing, *sorry.*

As I walk behind him to his car, I brace myself for what I'm assuming will be a very awkward car ride.

4
PAX

"This is your car?" Thomas asks as he pauses, standing a few feet away from Aphrodite.

"Mmhm," I mutter, pulling open the trunk to toss my gym bag in. I don't even bother trying to hide my irritation. First, he shows up in my first class *as my professor.* Then he shows up at my rugby practice with one of my teammate's girlfriends. And it was very fucking clear by the deer-in-headlights look on her face that she knew exactly who I was...in terms of my connection to Thomas at least.

I should have known, really. I knew Ayers was dating a professor. Naturally, she was friends with the one I just fucked. But this isn't going to be some double-date situation. No one on the team even knows I'm gay—except for Cullen now, I'm sure.

So when I slam the trunk closed and it echoes across the dark parking lot, Thomas gets the message.

"Listen, Pax..."

"Just get in," I mutter.

I do a quick scan of the parking lot to make sure no one else sees me taking a guy for a ride in my car. I know I'm being paranoid. Who would think we're fucking, just by me giving him a ride to the shop? But when you have a secret, something intimate about yourself, it's easy to feel like they already know. Like every little choice you make is a glowing neon sign that outs you without even realizing it.

Thomas doesn't hide his sexuality. He has a swagger that screams confident, gay man—and not just any gay man, confident *vers*. Which wasn't something I knew for sure yesterday so I had to take a gamble, not really knowing which way that was going to go.

And *fuck me*, he looks good. Especially in the passenger seat of my car. Against the faded dark brown leather, he looks like a fucking meal I want to devour. In fact, he looks too fucking good for me. Too perfect, crisp and clean. He has a wealthy, sexy energy that's designed to make me want him without ever really having him.

But I did have him. He let me fuck him yesterday, and he didn't even know my name.

It's a detail I loved, at first, but now as I realize this perfect man I'm suddenly pining for like a teenage girl with a crush is also a fucking whore, it makes me irrationally territorial. Does he just walk around letting everyone fuck him? Does he like it? Did I mean anything to him?

This is ridiculous. I need to avoid Thomas Litchfield at all costs, but how can I when he's sitting next to me smelling like heaven and looking like sin.

"I want to apologize," he says, as I rev the engine, pulling out of the parking space and moving toward the exit.

"What for?" I reply.

"Well, that's the thing. I don't know. Tell me why you're upset."

"Who said I'm upset?"

"Your behavior. The scowl on your face." He's being playful again, a slight lift to his lips.

"This is just my face." I shoot him a sideways glare, and his smile disappears. I don't know why I did that. Made him feel bad for bringing up my appearance. I'm just angry, but I honestly don't know why.

"I'm serious, Pax. Are you worried people will find out about you?"

"Find out what?"

"You know what."

"I don't. Why don't you spell it out for me, teach." Why am I being such an asshole? Fuck, even I don't know.

"Whatever. Look, it was an unlikely coincidence that I ended up being your teacher. I have no intention of telling anyone what happened last night and I don't plan on letting it happen again. We can just move on."

He sounds so cold and annoyed. I hate it, but he's right. We have to move on and forget each other. I can't be letting my secret out and having him around campus while anything is going on between us.

I could bring up the fact that he already told his friend about us. But I don't, because I don't want to fight with him. I don't want him to talk like that anymore. I miss the playful, flirtatious Thomas I met yesterday. But that chance is gone, so I might as well just stew in my disappointment.

"This is a nice car," he says after about five minutes of silence.

"Thanks."

"This is the kind of car you give a name," he replies with laughter in his tone.

I can't fight back the smile that's taking over his face. "Aphrodite."

"Oh, good one. I like it."

When I glance his way again, the stoplight in front of us illuminates his face in a bright glow that makes him look sexy as fuck. And with just that thought, my frustration is back. Nameless sex encounters are fine, especially for scratching a certain itch, but I hate the way I want to touch him again, want to dominate his body a second time.

I know it's fucking stupid, but I place all of the blame on him. It's his fault for being a whore, for being good looking, for being my teacher, for being in my car, and for being friends with my teammate and his girlfriend. How much I fucking like him is his fault too. My fingers squeeze around the steering wheel as I keep my eyes forward, refusing to expose my desire for him.

But the longer we sit in silence, the more the tension between us grows. By the time we pull into the lot of the empty garage, it feels like I'm driving a bomb that's about to detonate. I shift the car into park, but neither of us move. I can feel him readying to say something about what happened or how he's my teacher or some shit like that, some lame fucking grown-up shit that will sound more rational than I'm in the mood to hear.

So I don't let him speak. Instead, I reach across the seat and grab him by the back of the neck, jerking him toward me and crashing my lips against his.

There is not one ounce of fight in him. He opens for me like he did last night, but this time, it's his lips that part as we breathe hot air against each other, our tongues colliding in soft friction. A low groan rumbles from my chest, and my dick seems to remember how I made it shut up and wait this morning because it's eager to join the party now. I don't think it's ever hardened so fast in my life.

I don't usually like kissing. As a matter of fact, I can't remember the last time I kissed someone, but it's not for reasons having to do with the act of kissing or how much it turns me on. It's more of a self-preservation thing. If I let people kiss me, then they can feel the scars on my lips and cheeks, and I don't normally let people this close for that very reason.

But Thomas tastes *so...fucking...good*. I can't get

enough of his mouth. I pinch his bottom lip between my teeth, making him gasp and moan. My hands find their way to his crotch, and just like yesterday, he's right there with me. Pitching a pretty impressive tent —he's so turned on too.

My nerves are buzzing. I'm still full of the fury I had on the car ride to the shop, but my body and my brain are at odds. I want to squeeze this man so tight out of frustration it hurts. I want him to know how badly I *don't* want him. Or rather how badly I don't *want to* want him. Because I don't.

But here he is, being fucking hot and horny and always ready to go.

So I take him by the back of the neck and squeeze.

"Suck my cock," I demand.

He hesitates, staring into my eyes as his are darkened with lust. "Pax," he whispers. Then his eyes scan my face, seeing my scars up close, and I hate it. So I shove his face down to my crotch.

"I said, suck my cock," I repeat. I hate the way it sounds on my lips, so harsh and cold. This isn't me. I don't want to do this to him, but why can't I seem to stop?

He doesn't fight me. Instead, he tears down the waistband of my athletic shorts and pulls out my throbbing dick. His warm mouth breezes over my shaft, planting kisses from the tip down to the base, then licking his way back to the top.

My hand is still planted firmly on the back of his neck. "Don't fucking tease me," I growl.

His lips part and his tongue touches the head before sliding it in his mouth, gliding across the wet surface until I reach the back of his throat. He doesn't even gag as he coats my dick in saliva, closing his lips and bobbing up and down.

"Jesus," I mumble as my hips jerk upward to meet his movements. Using his hand at the base of my cock, where his mouth doesn't reach, he strokes me, squeezing on the upstroke. I can't stop watching him. He's so fucking perfect, and at this moment, he's all mine.

I rest my head back against the headrest and lose myself in the pleasure while he sucks and licks and squeezes. My eyes close and my grasp loosens, letting him take over. It's never been like this with anyone. Everything Thomas does is so flawless, and I almost don't want it to end.

I can already tell I'm going to get addicted to this, to him.

"Make me come with that perfect mouth," I growl, in a softer tone than before.

He hums around my cock as his lips tighten around me and he sucks even harder. He milks the cum out of me like a goddamn professional. I tighten my fingers around his neck as I jerk and unload into the back of his throat. The suction of his mouth doesn't stop until I'm wrung dry.

I melt into my seat, staring up at the ceiling as he lifts his face from my crotch, licking up the mess he made on my dick. I think I might die because I can't seem to breathe at all, and my heart feels ready to pound its way out of my rib cage.

When I finally relax a little, I look over at him. He's staring out the window, and I don't know if it's guilt or shame he's feeling, but I hate it either way. I don't want to be done with him yet. I want to yank him onto my lap and pepper his face with kisses, rub my nose in that beard of his, and then jack him until he paints my chest white, but I can't.

There is a wall between us. One we can peek over from time to time, but one I refuse to ever completely climb over. It's not an intentional thing, but this mental block I have will not allow me to be the least bit vulnerable. And telling this man how much I like him and want to see him again is exposing too much; it's too personal. All I have left is cruelty.

So I pull up my shorts, jump out of the car, and walk over to unlock the garage where his car is parked. It's a dick move, acting like I owe him nothing, and he will probably hate me for this, but that's for the best. Because I already hate myself enough for both of us.

5
THOMAS

He starts my car, and I watch him as he pops the hood to check a couple more things before declaring it's *good to go*. And that's it. He leaves it running, and waits for me to climb in and drive away.

I still have the taste of his cock on my tongue and he wants to act like he didn't just make me suck him off in the front seat of his car. Which seems to be a fucking habit of his.

There's not even a bill to settle, since they have my credit card on file, so there's literally nothing left to say as I climb into the driver's seat.

"See you tomorrow," I mutter as I adjust the seat to fit my height. When I glance up at him, he looks like he wants to say something, but he keeps quiet. Then, he slams my door shut, clearly telling me it's time to leave.

Sitting in the car under the bright lights of the garage bay, I watch him as he busies himself with cleaning up the shop. I'm still strangely hypnotized by him.

Finally, snapping myself out of it, I reverse out of the garage bay and drive into the dark night. It's a long quiet road back to the highway, giving me lots of time to think, so I relive the moment we just had in his car with his tight grip on the back of my neck.

I've had rough sex before. I've been told what to do and how to do it. I like it from time to time, but that's not what this was. Pax was mad at me. He wanted to hurt me. It turned me on—which is not something I expected.

But something is still bothering me.

He wants to keep me on a string, within his reach, but him out of mine. When he wants me, he takes me and then he immediately dismisses me, and it's not fucking fair. He's young, I get that. He's scared, putting up a wall, using distance as a defense mechanism, but it's not right. I deserve something more personal, or just *something more*.

"Fuck this," I mutter to myself as I slam on the brakes and spin the car around before reaching the freeway.

I'm not some fuckboy. Sure, I'm all for casual flings here and there, but I deserve a few words after. Not only that, I want more from Pax. In just two days, this kid has flipped everything upside down, and it's not fucking fair. I'm not usually so clingy to a one-night stand, but his utter disregard for me has triggered something in me, and I have too much to fucking say to walk away like this.

In the car, he wanted to play games with me. Pretend he's so unaffected, like nothing happened between us, and that probably pisses me off the most. He may be young, but he doesn't need to be so fucking immature.

God, what is my deal? I must be crazy, I think as I pull back into the lot of the mechanic shop. His car is still here, but the garage bay door is closed.

I waltz right past his car, and try opening the door to the shop, and I'm shocked to find it swings open easily.

"What are you doing?" a dark voice echoes through the empty garage. He's standing there in just his shorts and a T-shirt.

I march right over to him, ready to unload all of the things I've been piling up in my head on the drive back, but none of them quite make their way out in a coherent order.

"You can't...do this, Pax," I say with anger.

"Can't do what?" he replies in a clipped tone.

"Treat me like this. Like some fuckboy you can use and toss away. I'm not *that* guy," I yell.

"Okay," he says, and it's the casual nonchalance in his voice that sends me over the edge. He sounds like a bratty teenager, and it grates on my nerves.

"I'll admit. I was into it yesterday. I liked the quickie in the office and being what you needed at that moment, but now you're just..."

"Just what?"

"You don't want to talk about what happened at school? Fine. You want to be rough and fuck on the downlow? Fine. But you can't just walk away after and suddenly treat me like you hate me."

He has such a well-suited plate of armor on, it's infuriating. It's clear as fucking day that this is how Pax defends himself from emotions; he acts like it doesn't matter, and he doesn't care. And I don't see any way through that armor, so it's best to just walk away now before I'm in too deep and there's no going back.

"You know what...I don't care. I'll see you in class, but outside of that, there's nothing."

"Fine," he mutters.

I start to storm off toward my car, but something catches my eye. He's standing next to a thin foam mattress on the floor, and the thing in his hands is a pillow. He's wearing socks. But no shoes.

And the fight in me suddenly dissolves like paper in water.

He sees me looking and tries to step in my way to block me from seeing the proof that he's obviously sleeping in this filthy garage.

"Pax," I mumble, letting my eyes trail up to his face. His jaw tightens and he looks away. "Are you sleeping here?" I ask gently.

"I'm fine. It's just something I do from time to time. Have a good night, Mr. Litchfield," he mutters before turning to toss the pillow on the mattress.

Jesus, is this kid...homeless?

"Stop," I bark. As he glares up at me, his warm copper eyes soak up the fluorescent lights. "You can't sleep here."

"I told you, I'm fine. Now get the fuck out of here, please," he barks, and I can see how uncomfortable it is for him to show any kind of weakness.

I can't believe I'm even considering this—I just met this guy yesterday, but he's a student, and Everly and Cullen know him, so he's not a complete stranger. "Come stay at my place tonight."

"Just fuck off, Thomas."

Of course he's going to be a stubborn asshole. A little voice in my head says, *just leave him. He said he's fine and at least you offered.* But dammit, something about this guy catches me off guard. It's the scars and the wall he puts up that make me want to get through to him. It's the vulnerability I know he's afraid to feel and the fact that he's never going to make things easy for me, but maybe I'm tired of easy. Maybe I want a challenge and Pax Smith is definitely that.

Whatever the reason is, I'm about to stoke the flames that are already burning.

"If you don't take me up on my offer, Pax...I might accidentally forget to keep your little secret. I'd hate for the whole team to find out the truth."

He moves so fast it throws me off-kilter. His large hand is around my neck, and my back is slammed hard against the wall. His face is just inches from mine, his sneer so close to my cheek, I can feel the warmth of his breath on my skin.

"I hope you're not fucking blackmailing me right now, Mr. Litchfield."

"So what if I am."

"I said I was fine," he growls.

"Yeah well, I'm not. I can't just leave you here."

At this moment, he's actually quite intimidating. Towering over me, his body pressed up against mine, I'm dwarfed in comparison, but I'm not afraid of him. I think he wants me to be, and there's no doubt he could very easily hurt me, but I know he won't. I know that Pax Smith is far more cornered than I am. He's been abused or neglected and when threatened, he'd rather scare you away than risk being hurt again.

I want to help him, but the problem is, I don't know how to reach him. Behind this mean facade and scary exterior is a guy I know wants to be soft and maybe even taken care of. He started it with me. He could have literally watched me walk away without touching me yesterday, but he didn't, and I have to believe that me being older than him held some sort of appeal. Deep down, he needs someone like me. I just have to make him see it.

I gently wrap my hands around his wrists and coax him into releasing his grip on me.

"Come on," I say. "Let's make a deal. You call the shots, okay? You want to come to my house and have your way with me, okay. You want to tell me to fuck off and crash on my couch, okay. I'll leave you alone.

Want to be a dick to me in front of the whole class and the rugby team, just to be sure no one suspects anything? Fine. I don't care. You call the shots, Pax."

Finally, he lets go of my shirt long enough to let me breathe without the force of his body pinning me to the cinder block wall. But I don't let go of his wrists, at least not right away.

When I do release him, the anger drains from his face and he replaces it with confusion. "Why the fuck are you being so nice to me?"

Nice? This is a step above basic decency, but he must have had to deal with a lot of fucked-up assholes in his life to see this as me being nice. I don't really want to point that out, so instead I just reply, "Beats the fuck out of me."

6

PAX

I can swallow down the embarrassment of being caught sleeping in the garage. I can even handle the shame of taking charity from someone I barely know. What I can't fucking handle is Thomas being so fucking nice when all I've been is a complete asshole to him.

It feels like the more I try to push this guy away, the more he keeps coming back. I've been nothing but an ignorant, self-absorbed asshole since the moment I ambushed him in the office yesterday and fucked him without so much as a greeting.

I follow him to his place, which, of course, is downtown. It's a small condo, but I'm willing to bet he paid a shit ton for it. I feel so exposed when I park my car in his driveway. Aphrodite is not subtle. If people see it parked here, they will know it's me.

The minute we walk inside, I feel completely out of place, and I want to bolt. It looks like one of those fancy magazine homes without a touch of anything personal. I still have grease under my fingernails and this guy has a white fucking sofa. This is a nightmare.

The living room is off to the right with the kitchen at the back. To the left are the stairs leading to the second floor. Thomas walks in ahead of me, switching on lights and dropping his keys in a tiny white porcelain bowl by the front door. Meanwhile, I'm standing awkwardly in the entryway as he heads toward the kitchen. We still haven't said a word to each other since I had my hand around his throat.

I may have overreacted a little, but I don't like the feeling of being pressured or cornered into anything. And I especially don't like attention, which is exactly what Thomas seems to like to give me.

"Come on in," he calls from the pristine white kitchen. "Hungry? I'm not a good cook, but I can put something in the oven."

"I'm fine," I mumble, still standing by the door.

He watches me from under the bright lights, while I'm over here hunkering down in the shadows. It's silent for a moment and awkward as hell.

"The guest bedroom is upstairs," he says, moving toward the set of stairs. As he brushes past me, I breathe in the scent of his cologne, and my dick responds. He did say I could have my way with him, and sex would probably eat up some of the tension, but to be honest, I'm fucking beat. I slept like shit last night. Practice was exhausting, and I had a packed schedule today.

So without a word, I follow him up to the second floor. There is a room to the right that I can tell right away by the giant bed and clothes on the dresser that it's his. To the left, there is a bathroom and a spare room. Thank God the bedding is deep blue and not white. I don't think I could take anymore fucking white.

"Towels are in the hall closet. Help yourself to the shower. There are spare toothbrushes under the sink."

I only nod in response. I don't bother mentioning that I take my showers in the locker room after practice because that's fucking embarrassing. And I don't dwell too long on the fact that he has spare toothbrushes, because it means he must have a lot of overnight guests. Instead, I drop my backpack on the floor next to the bed and awkwardly wait for him to leave. After a moment of tense silence, he finally gets the message and tells me good night.

I don't bother to shut the door before I switch off the light and shed my clothes down to my boxers. I then flop down on the bed and melt into the memory foam mattress. The groan of pleasure that escapes my lips is loud. What this room lacks in personal touch, definitely makes up for it in comfort, and I hate to admit it, but this is much fucking nicer than a flimsy six-inch mattress on concrete.

After I hear Thomas shut himself in his room and the lights down the hall turn dark, I try to fall asleep. It takes a bit longer than I expected, especially considering how comfortable I am, but my dick doesn't seem to want to give up on the offer to 'have its way with him.' Luckily, my exhaustion wins and I'm deep in a dreamless sleep before I can act on it.

I wake up sometime before six. The house is quiet and cool, so I have no idea why I'm suddenly wide awake, but no amount of tossing and turning will let me fall back to sleep. I might as well just get up. I can slip out the door and go to campus early, so no one sees me leaving one of my professor's homes.

Before getting dressed, I sneak into the bathroom to pee, and when I come out, I see Thomas's bedroom door wide open. Curiosity gets the better of me and I tiptoe to his room to spy on him. There's a subtle blue glow from the alarm clock on his nightstand, and it illuminates his body on the bed. He's on top of the sheets, sprawled on his back in just his tight black boxer briefs.

Until now I've only been able to admire his body through the clothes he wears and the way his ass fills out a pair of tight slacks, but now I can drink in the ripple of shadows across his abs and his thick thighs in contrast to the white sheets. He's not a big guy, but the lean muscle of his body has my cock growing thick in my boxers.

Without making a sound, I give it a gentle stroke over my underwear. It feels heavenly as I stare at his sleeping form, the soft lull of his breathing the only sound in the house. It's intrusive of me, but I don't care. I need to come, and I probably *should* go do it in the privacy of the bathroom or the guest bedroom, but I can't peel myself away from him.

Plus, I'm breaking a pretty big rule of mine because I'm still half naked, and if he wakes up, he's going to see me. But then again this guy has me breaking all my rules.

Reaching under the elastic band, I palm the head of my dick, giving it a tight squeeze. It's hard to keep my groan silent, but I do, stroking myself while I watch him sleep. But even as I feel my orgasm building, I stop because I don't want to come in my boxers. Not before I get to touch him.

Silently, I cross the room and stand at the foot of his king-size bed. He's sprawled out on one side as if he's only taking up half of it in order to leave room for someone else. I'm tempted to crawl into the empty space, but I don't want to be next to him. I want to be *on* him. No, I *want* to be *in* him.

I slowly crawl onto the mattress, and he starts to stir, but he doesn't wake up. Straddling his lower legs, I drag my nose along one of his tan thighs while my hand slowly glides along the other, and it's not until I bury my face in the silky elastic of his underwear that I hear him hiss, and I know he's awake.

He's soft behind his boxers, but I feel the bulge of his dick and I wedge my teeth around it, giving him a subtle bite.

"Pax," he whispers in the darkness. His husky tone is laced with fear and arousal. Threading his fingers into my hair, he shifts his hips upward, pressing my face into his groin. With my nose buried in the fabric, I inhale his masculine scent. What is it about this guy that turns me on so damn much? It's like his pheromones are a drug to me.

He hardens quickly between my teeth, so I slide my fingers under the waistband and drag down his boxers to find his shaft. My first time really seeing it this close, I admire his impressive cock, like him slender and long. Naturally, it's perfect. Thick veins run along the underside, and I lap my tongue along each one. He gasps and moans, squirming on the bed as I tease him. The torture is fun, making him suffer in anticipation.

Then, wrapping my hand around him, I give him a couple hard strokes before taking him in my mouth, letting him glide as far down my throat as I can without gagging.

"Fuck, fuck, fuck," he groans, his back arching off the bed, and I already want to come just from the sounds he makes as I suck him off. His cock touches the back of my throat, and I bury my nose in the neatly trimmed hair around his shaft. My other hand finds his balls and gives them a gentle tug that stops his breathing altogether. Without letting up, I keep my momentum, dragging him closer and closer to his orgasm, knowing mine won't be far behind.

I've never gotten off from giving someone else a blow job, but my grinding hips against the mattress are leading me to believe this might be a first.

When I do feel his balls tighten under my fingertips, I ease up on his dick; I'm not ready to end this just yet. I want to draw out every second and make it last forever, especially in this twilight darkness before we've even spoken to each other today. It's like a clean slate, and I haven't had a chance to fuck it up yet. I want to enjoy it while it lasts.

But I can't help how good he tastes in my mouth, and I suck harder, moving faster and lapping up the drops of pre-cum he leaks onto my tongue.

When his balls tighten again, I know he's about to blow. But I don't let him come down my throat, not because I don't like to swallow but because I want his cum in my hand. Picking up speed and squeezing tighter, I take him to the very edge before pulling my mouth away. His body jerks and he lets out a strangled cry as the warm spurts fill my palm.

Before he can even catch his breath, I move upward onto my knees, pulling out my own cock and using his cum as lube to jack myself.

"Jesus," he gasps, watching me stroke my own cock. The wet sound of my hand around my shaft is filthy and sexy. He squeezes my hips, and his gaze doesn't leave my stroking hands. "Fuck, you turn me on so much. I love watching you do that." With his sexy, praising words, it doesn't take long before I'm shooting my load all over him. I can just barely make out the lust in his eyes as he stares at the movement of my hand.

It's dark enough that he can't really see me—or at least I tell myself that. Thomas seems to be pretty accepting of the shit all over my face, but I can't really hide it. I can hide my body, though, which I choose to do. I don't know how he'd react to seeing the rest of it, so as long as we're doing this, we'll stay in the dark.

After my cock is spent and I've wrung myself dry, I rub my jizz-soaked hand over his pecs, mixing our cum together over his chest hair. I feel his heart pounding as he tries to catch his breath.

I'm in a post-orgasm daze myself, so I don't even realize what he's doing until it's too late. He reaches over to the nightstand, and the lamp suddenly flicks on, bathing the room in soft, yellow light.

"Shit," I curse as I slump forward, but it's too late. He's already staring wide-eyed at my body, hovering over his.

"What's wrong?" he asks. "Are you okay?"

I refuse to run away or hide like a scared little kid, so instead, I lean back on my heels and let him see me. His chest is still covered in a sticky mess, but when his eyes cascade over my naked body, I don't think he cares about the cum coating his skin anymore.

"Fuck, Pax," he whispers. I can't look him in the eye, so with my jaw clenched, I keep my gaze focused on the wall. Then I feel his fingers trace the shapes on my chest. They are wide, pink, puckered scars that stretch from my shoulders to my waist in various directions. The beauty of growing to my size is that the scars I got from when I was six have grown with me. And I know how gruesome they look, a constant reminder of the world I was born into.

When I don't respond to his touch or look him in the eye, he seems to understand that I don't want to talk about it. His fingers drop away from my chest and land on my hips.

"Come shower with me," he says, slapping my ass playfully with one hand.

I'm about to say no and argue, but I don't. I'm not sure why, but I actually follow him to his en-suite bathroom and peel off my boxers at the same time he does. It's bright as fuck in here, but he doesn't stare at my body anymore. He takes my hand and pulls me under the cascading stream, and together, we wash our bodies without talking.

After our shower, we each get dressed, and while he's making his morning coffee, I slip out the front door. I don't ask to stay again, and he doesn't invite me, at least not yet. But I clearly need to make a plan that doesn't involve me sleeping on the floor because I could get used to staying at Thomas's house, and that would be a problem. A big fucking problem.

7
THOMAS

I don't have Pax's phone number. This occurs to me on the drive to campus, about an hour after he disappeared this morning. He took everything with him, but I sort of expected him to stay over again. He can't possibly plan on sleeping on the floor of the mechanic's shop, not when he has a perfectly warm and comfortable place to stay at my house. Something I'm offering out of the goodness of my heart, and not just because waking up with my cock down the throat of a six-foot-four rugby player is a lovely way to start the day.

And the sight of him jacking off onto my chest will be etched into my mind forever, giving me little sparks of pleasure all day long. He didn't seem to be a fan of the lights though, and I guess after seeing those scars, I can see why. I just wish I could have the Pax I get in the dark in the daylight too. Because when it's just us, and he's not worrying about what I see, it's actually kind of nice. We seem well-matched, like the same fire burns in both of us.

When he walks into class, I don't say anything to him. He ignores me and I ignore him. The class is a simple second-level English course, so there are a lot of students and not much time for class discussion. It makes the perfect environment for Pax to blend into the crowd and for me to pretend I don't know him at all, especially not intimately.

And everything is fine when he takes a seat in the back of the room, until a busty brunette with shorts cut so high I can see the crease of her ass cheek plops down into the chair next to him. It's not just that she sits next to him, it's the way she smiles at him after she does. And the fact that he smiles back.

Now, I am too old to get caught up in jealousy, and I certainly do not get jealous of girls who flirt with the men I'm interested in, but this one, for some reason, has my attention.

One of Pax's rowdy teammates comes in and drops into the seat on the other side of him. He's loud, striking up a conversation with Pax about practice yesterday and plans for the weekend. Pretty soon, the girl has joined in and the three of them are talking loud enough for the whole room to hear over the general chatter.

Pax is looking at me. His expression is heavy, lips tight and jaw clenched.

And I hate this for him. I hate that he has to pretend he's something he's not. I hate that life has thrown him so much shit that he's built armor around himself so he doesn't have to feel anything anymore. I hate that I want to get inside that armor when I know he'll never let me.

The girl touches his arm, and he sends her a tense smile. Not that I've seen a lot of Pax's smiles or know what the different ones look like. The first day in the car, though, I feel like I got a glimpse of what he's like with his guard down. As he talks to her, looking uncomfortable as he does, it makes me wonder how far he would go to prove his straightness.

When I glance down at my watch, I realize I'm five minutes late starting class, so I quickly get the students' attention and get started with today's lecture. Since this course is mostly geared toward writing, we get started with a short writing assignment students can complete in class. I give them fifteen minutes to answer the writing prompt on the board, which goes fine, except about two minutes into the exercise, the loudmouth next to Pax starts babbling on about some story from the weekend.

He's not really talking *to* Pax. It almost seems like he's talking to the girl on the other side of Pax more, but either way, it's disruptive and the fact that Pax is involved irritates me even more.

"Please keep quiet until the timer goes off," I say, but the rugby player only glares at me and continues whispering, without even doing it quietly. Of course, I can't remember his name—it being only my second day.

Pax is actually focusing on his writing, but after a few moments, he drops his pencil and I can tell he's frustrated with the guy next to him. But instead of telling him to shut up, he starts whispering along with him, and now I'm really irritated, which is unfair, considering the morning I had. All things considered, I should be in a great fucking mood.

So before the time goes off, I snap.

"Mr. Smith," I call. Everyone looks up, even Pax, who is staring at me with wide eyes. "I need you to keep it down or I'll have to ask you to leave."

"Are you fucking serious?" he mutters, and the class collectively gasps.

It feels like he's saying that to me as the guy he's currently fucking and not his professor, and I clam up, glaring back at him.

"Yeah, I am. Right now, it's class time. So act like it."

His eyes widen even more. The room is silent as he shoots daggers at me with the intensity of his stare. I've fucked up, I know it. I let my irritation, albeit irrational, mess with my judgment, but something about him carrying on with these two students bothered me.

Calling him out was wrong. The last thing Pax wants is attention. He's pissed at me, and I can already anticipate how he's going to make me pay for it.

Suddenly, the timer on my computer goes off, breaking the tense silence in the room. As I quickly shut it off, the students put their pencils down and wait for my instruction. Pax is still watching me from the back row, and I feel his eyes on me for the rest of the class.

When it's over, and the students start packing up, I decide I'm going to apologize to him. I'll ask him to stay behind, and it'll give me a chance to get his phone number anyway. I want to make it clear that he's welcome to stay at my place again, if it means he doesn't have to sleep on the ground. Out of the goodness of my heart.

And in hopes of another good-morning blow job.

But with the way he's glaring at me now, the chances of that are getting slimmer by the second.

"Do you guys have class after this? Want to go grab a coffee?" the brunette asks, as they start to shuffle their way down the aisle.

"Sure," the jock answers. "Pax?"

"I have another class."

I'm busy packing up my stuff and saying goodbye to the other students when I feel his eyes on me, and I wonder if he actually has another class or if he's making up an excuse not to have to talk to her anymore. I want to tell him that avoiding girls is going to give him away before being caught talking to me would.

"Mr. Smith, can I have a word?" I say to him as he passes by. The other students stare for a moment, and Pax just looks annoyed. He nods and waves to the others as they leave.

Then it's just us. We're alone, but the door is still wide open. He stalks toward it without a word, slamming it shut, making the hairs on the back of my neck stand up.

"Pax, I want to apologize," I say, but the words barely make it out of my mouth before he's shoving me against the wall. "I shouldn't have called you out like that."

"Let's get one thing clear, Mr. Litchfield," he says, when our bodies are flush, and I'm pinched between him and the wall. His face is just inches from mine. "You don't know me, and I don't know you. Don't talk to me, look at me, or touch me. I don't do relation-ships, so when we're alone, I own you."

His hand cups my dick forcefully, and I jump, but he doesn't let me move. The tighter he holds me in place, the harder I get under his hand.

"Oh, you like that, don't you, Mr. Litchfield?"

I stare into his eyes without flinching. This is really not my MO, the one being pushed around, bullied and talked down to. Not that I'm usually doing this to others, but the guys I normally date don't have the attitude or fire Pax does.

So why am I putting up with it now? Why do I let him talk to me like this? And why is my dick hardening so fast when I know I'm not going to let him fuck me here in this classroom. Not when he talks to me like this and refuses to open up to me. Whenever things get too personal for Pax, this is what he defaults to—pushing me around and trying to fuck me. All part of his defense, I know.

And I'm a stubborn mother fucker who wants to

get inside that armor. But the more I enable this kind of behavior, the more he's going to do it. It gets me nowhere. So instead of grinding into his hand like I want to, I relax against the wall.

"You're in charge, Pax," I say, holding my hands up in surrender. His expression falters for a moment, as I'm sure he wasn't expecting my concession. We stare at each other for a long moment, waiting for the other person to do something, when he does what I least expect—he kisses me.

It's soft and warm, his lips aren't hungrily searching for something or forcing my lips apart with his tongue the way he did in the car yesterday. He's kissing me like it's a language only we speak, a silent conversation. The hand on my crotch releases its hold and it drifts upward, snaking its way around my waist and pulling me closer. My hands are on his sides, running my fingers along the hard muscle of his body.

As his tongue slides against mine, he lets out a soft hum, and my fingers dig into his back.

"Come over tonight," I breathe against his mouth.

"Okay," he replies quickly before diving back in. The hand he was using to prop himself up against the wall digs into my hair, curving my body harder against his. I've never dated a man this much taller than me, and I've got to say, I fucking love it. He engulfs me, making me feel like a small plaything in the hands of a giant.

This kiss feels like it will never end, and I never want it to, but the sound of the heavy door being opened is like an alarm going off. Pax and I tear away from each other, our mouths both red and swollen from the kiss. We both position our bodies away from the door, so whoever is about to walk in doesn't spot the massive erections we're both sporting.

I'm prepared to be horrified at being seen alone with a student, but I'm actually massively relieved when Everly peeks her head in.

"Oh, hey," she stammers, quickly averting her eyes and ducking back out. "Sorry."

Pax looks horrified, and I can see the anxiety building behind his eyes. I touch his arm and give him a silent reassurance.

"It's okay," I whisper. Then I call out to Everly. "I'll be out in a minute."

"No rush," she replies. Pax still appears distraught.

"I'll see you later, okay?"

He hesitates as he glances at the door again, and my heart breaks for him. The closet he's put himself in is a prison of his own making, which means that only he can set himself free.

8

THOMAS

"I'd just like to start off this conversation by saying I won't even bother trying to talk you out of this," Everly says, as soon as Pax has disappeared and she and I are alone.

"Good," I reply, zipping my bag and throwing the strap over my shoulder. "Because that would be super hypocritical."

"I know," she adds, but I can tell by the tightness of her lips that she has more to say.

"But...?"

"But..."

"Just come out with it already, Everly. But do it while we walk because I need coffee. Or alcohol." It's only 10:00 a.m., so I guess I should stick with caffeine.

"I'm just worried about you, that's all."

"Worried about what?" I ask, locking the door to the room behind us.

"Promise not to bite my head off for what I'm about to say."

"Not a chance I'll be making that promise."

"Fine. I'll say it anyway," she replies, before scanning the hallway to make sure we're truly alone. "Thomas, you tend to get yourself more emotionally invested in these flings than you think you do."

"What?" I nearly shout as I glare at her. "I do not."

"Yes, you do. What about Nico?"

"What *about* Nico?" I snap back. I've only just noticed that he hasn't texted or called since I slept over at his place Saturday night, not that he normally does. In fact, he usually only contacts me on the weekends and not even every weekend. I know I'm a booty call to him, but usually by the middle of the week, I start to get anxious or irritated by his lack of communication.

"He's been stringing you along for two years, Thomas. And don't say it doesn't bother you that he only calls you for sex. I'm the one who has to listen to you complain about it."

Well, fuck. She's crazy if she thinks I'm going to fess up to that.

"I promise that is not what is happening with Pax. It was a one...or two-time thing, but I'm not getting emotionally invested in him like that. He's not even old enough to drink for fuck's sake."

"He's not even out yet," she replies in a low whisper. "Is that really something you want to be a part of?"

Fuck, no. I went through my own coming out when Pax was probably in diapers. It's not really something I want to relive, and I'm certainly not interested in going through that with the guy I'm dating either. Everly doesn't understand this thing with Pax, and honestly, neither do I.

We reach the coffee shop on campus and after we both order our drinks, I find a table for us while we wait. It's loud in here, bustling with students and music, so it's semi-private enough to carry on a conversation.

"Listen, I promise I'm not getting emotionally involved with him like that, okay?"

"What do you mean 'like that?'" she asks.

"I just mean that I feel bad for the kid. I mean, obviously he's had a rough life," I say, gesturing to my face, and she nods understandingly. "He's in the closet, and I mean...he's fucking homeless, Everly." I make sure to completely whisper that part, and her eyes go wide as I say it.

"Homeless?" she replies, ducking lower over the table, so no one can hear.

"Don't you dare repeat that to anyone, especially Cullen. It would only piss Pax off and I can handle it for now, okay?"

She nods in understanding, just as the barista calls our names. I quickly grab them from the counter and when I return to the table, Everly has a concerned expression on her face.

"Promise you won't say anything," I repeat.

"I promise, really."

"Then what are you thinking?" I ask.

She chews her lip as she adds sugar to her coffee. "I'm just thinking...poor kid. Cullen's only told me a little bit of what he knows, and I mean...he was dealt a really shitty hand."

I have to bite my lip because as badly as I am dying to know what Cullen knows, there's a part of me that only wants to hear it from Pax himself, as if he would ever open up to me.

"Do me a favor and don't tell me," I say. "Like I said, I can take care of it for now, but if I really think he's in trouble, I'll report something, okay?"

"Okay," she agrees. We sit in silence for a moment, and I can practically see the wheels turning in her head. Everly always has something to say. She's obsessed with right and wrong and justice whenever possible. But we live in gray areas that she just cannot seem to accept.

"Just say whatever you're thinking," I tell her.

"I don't want to. I'll jinx it."

A laugh bubbles up from my chest. "Since when are you superstitious?"

"I'm not. I was just thinking that...maybe this is exactly what you need."

"And what's that?" I ask, expecting her to say something like a tragic heartbreak to set me straight (not literally) or a tough rugby player to knock some sense into me. Instead, she drops a bomb of reality I wasn't prepared to hear.

"Someone who needs you."

And I don't know why that piece of truth hurts, like pouring salt on a wound I forgot I had, but all I can do is nod and pretend she didn't just say that. Is someone needing me the only way I can get them to stay with me? Or do I genuinely need to feel valued by the men I let into my life? Which of those applies to Pax? Does he really need me or is he just looking for a place to crash? I don't want to be a landing pad for some homeless twenty-year old with nowhere else to go.

But that's exactly what I'm doing, isn't it? Maybe because I'm actually starting to like this one. I like the idea that he needs me, but it scares me because what happens when he doesn't anymore?

9

PAX

The impact of my body slamming into the forward holding the ball is so hard it rattles my fucking skull, but he goes down, and the ball flies out of his hands, allowing my teammate to take possession.

"Good energy, Smith!" the coach calls from the sidelines. "Nice play!"

It just so happens that I'm full of enough pent-up energy and irritation today that my body is doing the job without having to think about it too much.

Slam that guy into the ground? No problem.

Knock this team off their feet? Easy.

Why am I so full of anger today? Well, it could have been that little stunt Thomas pulled during class this morning, calling me out when it was clearly Richards who needed the ass-handing. But he called on me, told me to act right, and that pissed me off. I might be his student, but I'm not his bitch and I don't play power-trip games.

Which I think he understood after class when he basically handed control over to me. And everything was good. Thomas has a way of knowing exactly what I need and giving it to me exactly when I need it. He makes everything so easy, and I'm starting to really fucking like him. He's easy to be around, even the silence is comfortable and he doesn't push me, even when I can tell he wants to do so.

But then Ms. West had to walk in, and even though it's one more person who knows my secret now, it feels like everyone does.

Thomas is in my head, and I know I need to just stop seeing him, stop going to his place and letting myself get away with what feels good and make the smart choice. He's getting too close, and once I let him in, I might as well just let everyone and everything in.

Is he worth it?

Fuck if I know.

After our Forward scores and the ref blows the whistle, we head toward the sidelines. Richards slams his heavy hand against my back. "Fuck yeah, Pax. That was a killer hit, man. You probably scared that Forward shitless."

Another player, Benson, laughs. "Big ugly monster running toward him like that. I'm surprised he didn't just hand us the ball."

I punch Benson in the shoulder. "Speaking of

ugly," I reply. "Tell your mom she left her panties in my car."

"Ohhhh," Richards bellows from next to me, and the team breaks out in laughter.

Benson has an ear-to-ear grin and it's fine. It's fine like this, laughing along with them rather than letting them laugh *at* me. I learned years ago that this is how you avoid the pain. Keep up the joke, let them have their fun, and don't take it personally.

My eyes glance in the direction of the stands, and I spot Thomas immediately. He's sitting next to Everly, and although she's watching with interest, he couldn't look more out of place. His eyes are fixated on his phone, and I know the only reason he's here is for me. At least I think it is.

I haven't spoken to him since after class. He invited me over again, and I'm telling myself I'm going there for sex, not because I literally have nowhere else to go.

As it turns out, beating the shit out of opponents on the field is excellent stress relief because by the end of the game, which we win by a long shot, I'm in a great fucking mood. I spot Thomas still sitting by Everly when I head toward the locker room. He gives me a very subtle head nod and I return the gesture. I find myself hoping he'll wait around for me while I shower, which is very unlike me.

On the walk toward the locker room, the opposing team passes us on their way to the bus. We don't say anything to them, but you can tell by the sour looks on their faces that they have some bitter resentment and hurt feelings. And I almost think we're going to get by unscathed when the guy I hit pretty hard in the first half turns around and calls toward us.

"Hey, number twenty-three, how long you been sucking the ref's dick?"

It's Mason Richards who spins around and grabs the player by the shirt. "What the fuck did you say to him?"

"I figured he must be smoking someone's pole since he never seems to get fouls called on him."

Mason only grips him tighter, and the guy looks ready to blow. His face is beet red, and he has such a deep scowl on his face, I know it means he's ready to throw down right here.

"Richards, stop!" I yell, grabbing my friend by the arm.

"You heard the faggot," the guy spits back in Mason's face, and I know shit is about to get ugly. I don't know why, at that moment, my eyes cast upward toward the stands and my gaze locks with Thomas's.

"Is he as fucking stupid as he is ugly?" the asshole in a vise grip asks, and I don't know why I snap this time. I've put up with all the names, all the insults, and I don't care what this ignorant piece of shit thinks about me, and I never take this stuff personally, but this time, it *is* personal. I see Thomas's face in my mind when I start swinging. There must still be a lot of pent-up rage coursing through my veins because my fist clobbers his jaw so hard, I feel a crack.

Then everything erupts into chaos. Both teams rally for their respective player and punches start flying. There's not a single person in this tornado of fists and elbows trying to stop it, and I lose sight of anything outside of this brawl.

I have the idiot who called me the f-word by the collar of his jersey, and I'm pummeling his face, when I feel a hand wrap around my arm, pulling me backward. I don't know how, but I register something familiar about the touch that's trying to hold me back, and while I could easily brush it off and continue breaking this guy's nose even worse, I let the hand stop me.

When I turn around and see Thomas standing next to me, wild fear and shock in his eyes, I immediately let go of the punk who started all this shit. Most of the guys are still amped up and fists are still flying, and Thomas sure as shit should *not* be here, least of all for me.

Suddenly, Benson comes flying backward, crashing into Thomas and landing an elbow right into his nose. I act on instinct, crowding Thomas and wrapping an arm around his waist to pull him out of the squall.

The coaches and security have finally broken up the fight, leaving the field in a strange aftershock of adrenaline and chaos. I pull Thomas away from the crowd and into the locker room. It's empty in here, so I drag him to the sink when I notice his nose is bleeding.

"Fuck. Are you okay?" I ask.

"I'm fine," he mumbles. I grab a handful of paper towels and press them against his nose, tilting his head back to stop the bleeding.

"You took a punch too, you know," he says, nodding up toward my eyebrow. A quick glance in the mirror and I see the blood trickling from a gash above my eye.

"I'm used to taking punches," I say.

My hands are wrapped around his face, holding him closer than a straight man would hold another man. Then it finally registers that anyone could walk in here at any moment, and I truly don't know if I care. Maybe it's the adrenaline or maybe I'm just tired of hiding something I shouldn't be ashamed of.

"What made you snap like that?" he asks.

I take a minute before answering, thinking back to that moment when I lost control and decked the guy in the face. I know I hit him hard, probably harder than I've ever punched anyone, and I know it must have hurt like a bitch, but it couldn't possibly hurt as bad as being called ugly and stupid your entire life. And I can now add faggot to the list.

That one shouldn't hurt, but it does. It hurts because I don't feel shame for being gay. It hurts because out of all the shit I've put up with in my life, I'm looking into the eyes of the first guy who makes me feel good, and I hate the idea that someone could make that a bad thing.

"I don't know," I tell him, and it's true. I don't

know why all of a sudden I'm triggered by the shitty things people say to me. I think Thomas has gotten into my head, made me realize I don't deserve it or something. Like maybe if a guy like him likes a guy like me, I'm not such a piece of shit after all.

We hear the guys coming before we see them, so I quickly let go of Thomas's face and back away. The whole team crowds the locker room, followed by Coach Johnson, who looks steaming mad.

"I'll get out of here," Thomas says before tossing the bloody towel in the garbage. He quickly ducks out through the crowd of rowdy, sweating, bleeding rugby players.

I immediately catch the way Richards is watching him. Then his eyes suddenly land on me, and I feel like I have it written on my forehead. *That's the guy I'm fucking.*

The coach gives us a verbal ass whooping about learning to keep our cool and letting shitheads like the guy on that team be shitheads. It's a whole *be the bigger man* speech, and I feel like it's directed at me. I always keep my cool. I am *always* the bigger man, but this time, I fell victim to the anger because it's not fucking fair. It's not fair that he can be a dick, but I have to let it slide. I'm fucking tired of it. Of all of it.

After Coach's done giving us hell, we hit the showers, and by the time I exit the locker room, it's dark outside. Crossing the parking lot, I notice there's no sight of the familiar BMW I want to see waiting for me. And I hate how disappointed I feel.

In just three days, I've gotten myself stuck on this guy. Now at least one to three people know the secret I wasn't ready to reveal. So as I climb into my car, I know what I should do. And it's not even close to what I want to do. Or what I actually do.

10
THOMAS

It's past ten, and he's still not here. After the moment in the locker room, I was sure things were good between us. He didn't seem to care so much about hiding our relationship when he was hauling my ass out of that brawl and into the locker room. I figured he would come over after his shower, so I didn't bother waiting for him. I didn't want to make things too obvious.

Now I'm second-guessing myself. Did he think my leaving was my way of saying I didn't want him to come over? Am I thinking about Pax far too much for a guy I just met a couple days ago? Definitely. Does that stop me? Absolutely not.

I should go to bed. Pretend it doesn't bother me whether Pax comes over or not or where he chooses to sleep tonight. It's none of my business. He's just a student, a guy I've had a couple sexual encounters with this week.

I make it to my bedroom, where I'm supposed to be getting into pajamas, but I can't move because he's not here, and I truly expected him to show up. There's only one place I know he could be, but if I check and he's not there, then it really is out of my hands, and I'll need to let it go.

So, I get in my car and drive the eight miles off the freeway to the mechanic shop. The garage bay is closed, but I can see a light on through the window panes along the top of the garage. After getting out of my car, I march up to the door and bang on it.

"Pax! Open up!"

I hear movement on the other side, but he doesn't open it right away.

"Pax!" I yell again and continue to bang. "What the fuck? You can't just ghost me like that!"

"I didn't ghost you," he replies from the other side. I'm relieved to hear his voice, to know he's actually here and I'm not yelling to no one or even worse, a complete stranger.

"Can you open the door so we can just talk?"

"Go home, Thomas."

"Why? What happened? Is this about the fight? About what that guy called you? Because he's a fucking idiot, Pax. He doesn't have two brain cells to rub together, so don't let him ruin your night."

"It's not about him," he groans.

"Then what is it about?"

It's silent for a moment before the heavy door starts to rise. On the other side, Pax stands there in sweatpants and no shirt, giving me an uninhibited view of his scars again, and I wonder if maybe he's doing it on purpose. It's like he's trying to remind me of who he is and what is wrong with him, and I'm not sure how to make him understand that there is *nothing* wrong with him.

"I don't want a relationship, Thomas," he says, holding the garage door open above his head. He's nothing but biceps and traps, and my mouth actually waters with the need to touch him.

"That's my line," I reply, which is almost funny. Because that is normally the game I play, but this time, it doesn't feel the same, and we both know it. When he doesn't react to my almost-joke, I continue. "I get it. Things have moved fast between us. It's been a hell of a week. I'm not trying to rope you into a relationship, but if there's something good between us, why are you running from it?"

He nods toward the shop behind him, and I walk inside so he can shut us both in, away from the cool fall breeze. It's unusually brisk tonight. There is a makeshift bed on the floor that looks like a thin foam pad covered in blankets. Nearby, a space heater is humming, which explains why it's a bit warmer in here than I expected.

Keeping his back to me, he walks over to the tool bench and busies himself by putting things away.

"I'm not running from it," he replies. "I'm just being cautious."

"This isn't cautious, Pax. It's resistant."

"Why do you even care?" he yells back, starting to get defensive. "You act like this with all the guys you hook up with?"

"No, I don't. Can't I just like you? Is that so hard to believe?"

"Well, we had our little hookup. Now let it go," he says, turning toward me without looking me in the eye.

"I don't get you. Today in the classroom, it was all about how you owned me, and I was okay with that. Then, in the fight, you wanted to protect me. But now...you want to call it quits."

"Yeah, I guess I just changed my mind."

He still won't look me in the eye.

"You know what I think? I think you didn't expect to like me as much as you do, and I think you really wanted to come over tonight, but it scared you because if you came, you might get used to it, and you might start to like it. And then someday, I might fuck you over like everyone else has and you're afraid of losing something good, so you choose to live alone and be miserable instead."

"You don't know anything about my life," he replies, charging straight for me. I don't cower as he stands toe-to-toe with me. His eyes are dark and fierce, glaring down at me with frustration. His nostrils flared and his jaw clenched.

"So tell me," I say. "Tell me why you're living on the floor of this garage and why you're alone and where you got the scars."

"Trust me, you don't want to know," he replies with a sarcastic laugh.

"Yes, I do."

The garage grows quiet for a moment as he stares into my eyes, and I wait for him to tell me to fuck off, which is what I'm sure is going to come out of his mouth next. Instead, he takes three steps toward me, forcing me back until I hit his car.

"Fine. You want to hear the story? Well, here you go. My mother was a drug addict and one night when I was eight, she got so high, she thought I was trying to kill her, so she attacked me with a knife from the kitchen. I was bleeding and cut up so bad when the ambulance finally arrived, they couldn't take my vitals, and they thought I was already dead."

"Jesus," I whisper. My hands drift up to his chest, and I touch the long white lines that stretch across his chest. Something in me cracks and splinters at knowing his story, knowing the reasons behind his scars. I knew whatever it was it had to be bad, but to know it was his own mother...

"And since I didn't have a dad, I bounced around foster homes for the next ten years, where the other kids were afraid to sleep in the same room as me because they thought I was a monster."

"Pax..."

"And to top it off, I realized about five years ago that I like dick instead of pussy, which wasn't such a bad thing to be honest because most girls were disgusted by me as it was."

He's worked up, the words streaming past his lips without caution, and I realize this might be the first time he's ever really spoken about any of this to anyone.

"Pax," I say again. He's towering over me now, so close it feels as if our bodies are fused. My hands move up from his chest to his face, where I cup his jaw and stare into his eyes. But he's not done. His abysmal, beyond sad story doesn't seem to end.

"I'm alone because my mom was sick, and I don't have any other family or friends. I only have my car and rugby, and that's all I need. I don't need a fucking boyfriend—"

Before he can say another word, I pull his mouth to mine, and he doesn't pull away. He sinks hungrily into the kiss, piercing my mouth with his tongue. Holding me tight, with his large hands on my back, he lets our kiss drown out the words that still hang in the air.

I want to kiss away every single thing he said. I want to wipe out the memories and the pain. If he needs my body to forget, then I'll give it to him. I have never in my life wanted to heal someone else so much, but I remember what Everly said today over coffee. I want someone to rely on me, and I realize how true that is. I want Pax to need me like air. I want to be the oxygen that fills his lungs and the person who provides a roof over his head.

And that is exactly how he's kissing me now, like he would die without it. I know in some way, this is the most vulnerable thing Pax has ever done, opening up, even the smallest amount, to someone else.

Our kiss grows more heated as my hands explore the planes of his back and chest, hungry for every touch. My lips move from his, down to his neck, nipping and licking every inch. I have never felt so starved for another person in my life. He hums when my mouth reaches his collarbone. His hands dig into my hips, grinding himself against me. When my kiss reaches his chest, I expect him to pull away or stop me, but he doesn't.

He lets me trace the scars with my mouth, kissing my way along each stretched-out mark. I want to rewrite his story, erasing the trauma and replacing it with this—something good. Something where he can feel accepted, wanted, valued...loved.

Without warning, he hooks his hands around my thighs and lifts me off the ground, setting me on the hood of his car. He's hard behind his sweatpants, and I reach for him, wrapping my hand around his shaft and stroking him through the fabric. He lets out a groan as his mouth devours my neck, earlobe, and jawline.

This moment feels like everything. It feels like I've been waiting for years for someone else to be as alive and as ravenous as Pax is. Someone I don't have to tone myself down for, but who matches my energy and hunger.

His fingers fumble with the buttons of my jeans, finally getting them open and eagerly reaching in for my rock-hard dick. After one stroke with his dry palm, he lets go and holds out his hand, spitting into the center before grasping my cock with his now saliva-soaked palm. Pleasure jolts up my spine like lightning.

I drag down the elastic of his sweatpants, eager to hold him, ecstatic to see he's as hard and as aroused as I am. Dragging my ass to the edge of the car, he holds me closer, leaning over me until our cocks are aligned, and then with one large hand, he engulfs them both, stroking them as one. His dick is warm and smooth against mine, and it feels incredible. My hips jerk along with his thrusts, and it makes what I want from him that much more potent.

I want to fuck him. I want him panting beneath me, crying out my name as I take him to the edge where pain and pleasure collide.

"Pax," I whisper into his mouth while he jacks us together. I don't know how he will take my request. There's a chance he'll freak out and bolt. Or he could just tell me no, and that would be fine, but I have to say it. Because this moment feels perfect. He *feels* like mine.

"What?" he gasps in return, as he pinches the heads of our cocks together, making my body jolt in response.

"I want to fuck you," I mumble against his lips. He tenses for a moment, but he doesn't stop, and he doesn't pull away. Instead, he kisses me deeper. It feels like a yes, and I'm nervous about it. I can't ask again, so if he doesn't say yes, that's fine. As long as I have him in whatever way I can.

As he pulls away from this breath-stealing, heart-stopping kiss, he lets go of our cocks and holds my face in his hands. "I want you to fuck me."

I swear all the blood in my body courses straight down to my cock, and it lights up every little nerve ending like I'm on fire.

"But..." he continues without taking his lips from my face, "I've never bottomed before."

Jesus. Fuck. I grab onto his hips and tug him closer. I can't even remember the last time I was with a first-timer, and maybe I should feel something more about it, but all I have is this overwhelming need to claim him, to truly make him *mine*.

He quickly tugs my shirt over my head and lifts me again, carrying me over to the mattress on the floor. Not exactly the sex destination of my dreams, but right now, I only care about him and being inside him as soon as humanly possible.

Our clothes come off in a rush, thrown haphazardly across the room until we are both naked, and I don't even care that it's still chilly as fuck in here. He's currently hovering over me, my own personal blanket of muscle and flesh, so I'm keeping plenty warm. I love that we're taking our time with each other. The last time we fucked, it was fast, and although it was hot as hell, I want to draw this out and explore every inch of him. He seems to have the same idea as he sucks on the skin of my neck, leaving what I'm sure will be a mortifying hickey on my neck, but oh-fucking-well.

I'm holding his cock in my hand, stroking him and

reaching for his balls with the other. The groan that he releases as I squeeze his sack echoes through the empty garage. Pax likes a little bit of bite to his pleasure, just enough pain to bring him to the edge.

"Get on your back," I say, my voice like gravel.

In the next heartbeat, he rolls us together until he's beneath me, and I move quickly down to his cock, swallowing the length in one quick motion.

He groans again, deep and raspy, as he digs his fingers in my hair, lifting his hips to meet the back of my throat. I gag, coughing as I come up for air.

"Oh my god, do that again," he moans. So I let him deep throat me again, cutting off the air to my lungs as he punches the back of my mouth. His cock is coated with saliva as I stroke him with my lips and tongue. I feel the head swell after picking up speed, so I slow down. I'm not ready for him to come just yet. Without taking my mouth off of his shaft, I squeeze his balls with my fingers again, feeling his legs tremor around me as I do.

Then I massage the velvety soft skin behind his balls, and his muscles jerk, but I know he likes it because he forgets to breathe for a minute. Pulling away from his cock, I dip two of my fingers in my mouth, coating them with spit as he watches me, eyes hooded with lust and anticipation. His lips are parted and he's staring at me like he's about to combust.

This time when I stroke his cock with my mouth, I rub my wet fingers around his tight hole. His legs fall open, and his breath comes out in a mumbled curse.

"Fuck."

And when I breach the ring of tight muscle, his head falls back and he makes a drawn-out noise that sounds like he's dying and loving it at the same time. Keeping my mouth on his cock, I work him open, first with one finger and then with two.

His body begins to rock with my movements, wanting more and needing me deeper. How he hasn't blown his load down my throat yet, I have no idea. Oh, to be twenty again.

"We're gonna need lube, baby," I whisper, kissing the inside of his thigh.

"Glove compartment," he barks out in a breathless gasp.

Leaving him on the floor, I jump up to retrieve it from his parked car. I've done it in some pretty unique places, but on the floor of a mechanic shop, surrounded by the scent of grease and smoke, this is definitely a first. As promised, there is a small bottle of lube and a pack of condoms in his glove box. Bringing both back, I find him lying on the mattress, sprawled out and stroking himself while he waits.

God, he's so fucking beautiful.

His shoulder-length dark hair is fanned out behind him, and when I stare at him in the bright fluorescent lights, I almost can't believe how unbelievably attracted to him I am. With those sharp cheekbones and broad, muscled shoulders. It's not that I don't see the scars—I won't pretend they're not there, but his scars make him fucking beautiful. Where they came from is ugly, and the fact that he endured that pain is disgusting, but him...this masterpiece of perseverance and survival is fucking breathtaking.

"What?" he asks, waiting for me to come to him.

"Nothing—I just like looking at you."

"Well, stop looking and start fucking," he says with a sinfully sexy smile on his face.

"Yes, sir," I reply, dropping to my knees between his open legs. I'll let him think he's in charge now, but he's about to be all mine.

11

PAX

I'm not nervous. I'm just...impatient, and Thomas seems to think I need all the gentle prepping and warming up that I certainly didn't give him when we fucked before. Kneeling between my legs, he covers his fingers with the lube from my car, working me open again, and it's fucking heaven. The burn, the pressure, the new sensation. I need *more*.

"Just fuck me already," I grunt out, reaching for him.

But this fucker likes to drive me crazy. I can tell because instead of doing what I just said, he smiles wickedly and curls his fingers. My hips jack off the floor, and I have to squeeze the blankets between my fists as pleasure hits me so hard, I lose all ability to breathe.

"I swear to God, Thomas, if you don't fuck me soon..."

He has the audacity to laugh, a deep, sexy chuckle before finally pulling his fingers out of my ass and reaching for the lube again. As I watch him wrap up his dick and cover it with lube, I catch myself admiring how sexy this man is. I'm secretly jealous of the confidence he constantly exudes. He's smart, good-looking, and funny, and all without fucking trying. I should hate him, but for some goddamn reason, he wants *me* and that's something too irresistible to avoid.

After shoving a pillow beneath my ass, he lines himself up, pressing in the blunt head of his cock, and I take a deep breath. Before he pushes inside me, he leans his body over mine, and he lays a soft kiss against my collarbone just as he works his way in. The air is punched out of my lungs, and my fingers dig into the skin of his hips. The pressure is exquisite.

His lips find mine, and his tongue pierces my mouth as his dick thrusts in even deeper, until I can feel his balls slap my ass. And he keeps kissing me, even as he slips to the end, only to thrust all the way back in seconds later.

"You good?" he whispers.

I nod without hesitation, looking into his eyes. He plants his hands on either side of my head, and my fingers cascade down his rib cage like keys of a piano. Having him so deep inside me makes me feel even closer to him, like we are truly connected.

I could never let anyone else in like this, but I'm not so afraid with Thomas. I trust him.

"Fuck me," I groan, arching my back and tilting my hips to find that magic spot that just made my body light up like a Christmas tree.

He leans down and kisses me deeply again before lifting up until he's upright on his knees, staring down at me and the place where he's balls deep inside my body. He's watching himself fuck me, and as he starts to pick up speed, slamming in harder and harder, the pressure builds.

"You're mine," he growls as he fucks me. Fingers bite into the flesh of my thighs as he thrusts. I can't stop staring at him, fucking me like he owns me, dominating my body and making me feel pleasure I've never known before.

When I reach for my cock, knowing that I'm fucking close to blowing, he quickly swats my hand away with a hard slap. Pounding even harder, he takes my dick in his hand, squeezing it so tight, I lose control.

"Say it, Pax. Tell me you're mine."

"I'm yours," I groan.

"Get on your knees. I want you from behind," he commands, and goosebumps erupt all over my body. When he pulls out, the pressure is gone, and I immediately want it back. Flipping over to my knees, I wait for him.

His hand glides along my spine, pressing my shoulders down, and I lower to my elbows, just as he presses his cock back inside me.

"You're so big, Pax. And you're all mine." He slams in again, harsh and unforgiving. He's teasing me. With every thrust, my body is assaulted with need and overwhelming sensation, my cock bobbing with the momentum. But I don't touch it yet, because when I do, it'll be over.

"Please fuck me. I'm not going to last long," I groan.

He lets out a heavy breath behind me, his hands tight on my hips as he picks up speed. "God, you take my cock so well. I want to come, Pax."

Our groans and cries fill the room, mingled with the filthy sounds of our bodies slapping together, and it's fucking amazing. It's not even over and I already want to do it again. My hips rock backward to meet his thrusts.

"You first," he says in a deep breathless tone as he reaches around to grab my aching cock. The first squeeze is like torture; it's so fucking good, but I need to come.

He slows his thrusts as he jacks me, fast and hard. I can't stop the current as it hits me, making me cry out in a low moan that nearly shakes the walls of the garage. Warm jets of cum land on the mattress and I swear I see stars with the intensity of my orgasm.

His teeth dig into my back as I shudder. "Fuck, I love watching that."

Letting go of my cock, he grabs my hips and thrusts hard a few more times before riding out his own climax. I can feel his cock shake out his release inside me, and I never want him to pull out.

We both collapse, and I turn onto my back so he can lie in my arms, neither of us seeming to care that there's a mess beneath us. He kisses my neck between each gasp for breath.

"Oh my god," I say with a deep sigh.

"Oh my god is right," he replies, and we both laugh. It sounds like we just finished a ten-mile run with the way we're panting.

I'm disappointed when he leaves my arms, jumping up to discard the condom in the bathroom trash. I hear the water running as he cleans himself up, and now that I can finally take normal breaths, there's a strange burning smell that I didn't notice earlier. Glancing around the room, nothing looks out of the ordinary, so I assume it's coming from outside.

A moment later, he brings a paper towel to the mattress, cleaning up the mess we made and dropping a kiss to my collarbone when he's done. After tossing the dirty paper in the trash can, he drops onto the mattress next to me. He slips easily into place against my chest, his head lying comfortably on my shoulder. I'm letting myself relax when I'm with him, and it's hard to believe that something that started just a few days ago has suddenly ripped my reality into shreds, in the best possible way.

"I'm sorry for not coming over," I mumble against his temple.

"I get it. You don't have to apologize." He sounds

tired, like he's only a few minutes away from sleep. I should switch the lights off, but I hate the thought of him sleeping on the floor all night. "Promise you'll just sleep at my place until you get on your feet, okay?"

"Okay," I reply, kissing him again.

His fingers trace the shapes on my chest, and it feels nice. I couldn't tell you the last time someone even touched my chest, so the fact that I can let him do it and actually enjoy it is pretty remarkable.

I start to drift off at some point but then I'm jolted awake by the sound of breaking glass. Thomas and I startle at the same time, first staring at each other and then looking around the room for the source of the sound. Something hits the garage door with a loud smack. In the distance, there is laughter and the rumble of a car engine.

"What the fuck," I bark as I jump up, grabbing my sweat pants off the floor of the garage. I throw them on in a rush and bolt for the side door that leads to the street. I hear Thomas shouting, "Where is my shirt?" as I reach the door. I register that something is very off about the smell in the air and the hint of smoke, but I'm too distracted by the assholes standing in the middle of the dark street with large rocks in their hands.

Instantly, I recognize the guys from the game today, and rage boils to the surface so fast, I nearly black out. I hear Thomas running out behind me, and I turn to find him standing in nothing but his jeans.

"Oh, shit!" the guys yell. "He really is a fag."

I take off in a sprint toward them, not even caring that I'm not wearing shoes and the asphalt is biting at my feet. They're too far ahead of me to catch them as they dive into the back of their truck and it speeds away.

"Smoke, Pax!" Thomas yells from behind me. "Pax, something's burning in the garage!"

At first I think he must be confused or mistaking the smell of a distant bonfire I noticed before, but as I turn around and see the smoke billowing out of the broken window, my heart plummets to the concrete.

"What the fuck!" I shout as I run back toward the building. I grab the bottom of the garage door and pull it up, and I'm hit with a blast of smoke and heat. All I see is Aphrodite being swallowed up in a gray cloud and the flicker of a flame along the back wall.

"Help me!" I scream as I run toward my car, but a hand hooks around my arm, stopping me.

"You can't go in there!" he shouts.

"I have to get my car out!"

"No, Pax. We have to call 9-1-1. Forget the car."

"You don't understand!" I shout back, my body coursing with adrenaline and fear and so much anger. "That car is all I have."

I yank my arm free of his grasp and run into the smoke-filled garage. I trip over our makeshift bed on the floor. How long would we have slept through this?

As I reach the door of the car, swinging it open, I spot the space heater in the corner of the garage. It's my space heater. I'm the one who brought it, but it's

Thomas's shirt draped over the top, almost all of it unrecognizable by the way it's scorched. Something in me spoils at the sight.

Suddenly he's there, on the other side of the car, opening the door and getting in position to push it out of the garage, but I can see the annoyed scowl on his face.

"Put it in neutral, and let's push. Make it fast!"

Together, we roll Aphrodite out of the garage, and as soon as we get her a safe distance away, I throw it into park and run back toward the garage to grab the fire extinguisher near the door.

Thomas watches from behind me as I douse the flames. It goes out quickly, leaving the whole building a smokey mess. And as I stare at what's left, I know I'm fucked. The mattress is still on the floor, Thomas and I are stuck out here half-naked, and I'm 100% sure that I'm most definitely going to lose my job.

"Fuck!" I yell, scraping my fingers through my hair. It all happened so fast, the guys throwing rocks through the window, the fire starting. And right now there is so much rage and frustration coursing through me that I know I'm about to blow.

"Relax. At least we got out safely."

"Relax? Everything is ruined! I'm going to lose my job. I almost lost my car, and all because I had to be so stupid!"

He reaches for me, and all I see is his bare chest, evidence of what we've done. Evidence the cops and firefighters and my boss are going to see when they get here.

"Pax," he says, but I quickly jolt away from him.

"No. A week ago, everything was fine. And then you got in my head and I had to let my guard down. Now everyone is about to know. And who knows how much trouble I'm going to get in for this."

"So this is my fault?" he asks, looking shocked.

"You just had to intervene. You thought you were saving me, but you were just making everything worse!"

"How exactly did *I* make things worse?" he shouts back.

"It was your shirt on the space heater! It was because of *you* I got in that fight today and *you* who all the guys on the team saw me touching. And now all of those guys saw you here with me," I say, gesturing toward the road where the assholes drove off.

For the record, I know I'm being insanely irrational. I know Thomas can't actually be to blame for any of this, but this week has turned into a wildfire, and he was the one who lit the match.

"You realize none of that is actually my fault, right?" he asks in a cool tone.

"You don't understand, Thomas! This is why I don't even try. This is why I don't get along with people because they turn into assholes like those guys, and no matter how hard I try, the minute I let my guard down and think for one second that everything will be okay, it turns to shit! I wish you had never walked into my life in the first place."

He grinds his teeth together and glares at me. The hurt on his face destroys me because just ten minutes ago, I held him in my arms and everything felt *so good*. And I'm ruining it. No, I'm sabotaging it. I'm making sure that there is no trace of hope left.

"You know...it's not actually gone to shit just because one bad thing happens, Pax. And is everyone finding out who you really are so bad? Is it so bad if they know that the person you're with is me?"

"It was never going to work," I reply darkly.

"I guess not." The surrender in his voice hurts like hell.

It's silent as he stares at me, anger and confusion on his face.

"Just go home, Thomas."

"Why? Because things were good?" I wish he was as used to disappointment as I am because I can hear the emotion in his voice.

"I'm not going to be your fuck boy to boost your fragile ego," I yell, and I regret every single word. It's almost impossible to force the words out, but it's better this way. The sooner he leaves, the sooner he gets over me and realizes this was nothing more than a short fling. I don't want to admit feelings were involved or that I spilled every dark secret to him. I'd rather just pretend none of it happened at all.

I'm such a coward, I can't even look at him as he gives one last pissed off glare and spins to walk away. I ignore the sound of his car driving away as I call 9-1-1. And as I sit on the curb, waiting for the truck and my boss to show up, I try to pretend none of this happened. What I wouldn't give to go back to the lonely, pissed-off life I lived just four days ago, but I know there's no chance of that happening now.

12
THOMAS

Two weeks later

"I brought you something," a cheerful voice sings from the doorway of my classroom after it's emptied. I'm lingering to grade papers and sulk.

"What is it?" I ask, sounding entirely too depressed. "And I swear if you say Pumpkin Spice Latte...so help me..."

"Full fat, extra-whip Pumpkin Spice Latte with a caramel drizzle."

Everly dances her way down the aisle with two large coffees in her hands, and I can't help but at least crack a small smile as she sets one on the table in front of me.

"These are disgusting," I say, cracking the lid and taking a whiff. And I'm not just saying that because

I've become a serious buzzkill these past two weeks. She knows I hate PSLs but will indulge in at least one a week from September to December. I call it corporate brainwashing. She calls it a sugar and caffeine addiction. Either way, they're terrible.

"Thank you," I say, licking up the cinnamon-dusted whip cream.

"You're welcome." She pulls up a chair and sits on the opposite side of my desk. "So... big plans this weekend?"

"Not even a little bit," I reply. "You?"

"The guys have an away game Saturday. I think we'll be ordering pizza and hanging out at home tonight. You should come over."

Tilting my head at her, I send her an unimpressed glare. She's been trying to get me to come over *casually* every damn night since the incident with Pax. Why? Because Pax has been taking up residence in their guest bedroom since the fire, and apparently hasn't been in too good of a mood either. She tells me how he sulks and how Cullen is tired of the way he's been playing in their games, like a giant, stoned elephant—his words, not mine. I can't seem to get her to understand that that's just who Pax is. He is more comfortable in misery because it's what he's used to. I tried to pull him out of it once, and he didn't appreciate it.

"Call me when they leave," I say, and I can feel her disappointment permeating the air like bad perfume.

"You know...you did try to warn me," I say,

glancing up at her over my coffee. "You told me not to get emotionally invested."

"I know, but..."

"And it didn't work out. On the bright side, at least this one didn't drag me down a long two-year fuck-buddy relationship. But it's going to take me some time to get over it, okay?"

She nods, biting her lip. There's more she wants to say; I can tell. Ever the commentator, my friend, Everly. There is not a matter, public or private, that she can keep her opinions away from. It's a good thing she's my best friend or I swear, I'd get really sick of the way she thinks she knows best all the time.

"I wish you didn't have to get over it though."

"Yeah, me too," I mumble so quietly she probably didn't even hear it. "But as it turns out, dating a twenty-year-old student can't work out for all of us."

"Pax has put you through a lot less than Cullen put me through."

"And you chose to stick it out. I, on the other hand, am not going to test fate again. Pax doesn't want to be vulnerable and open up to people, and I don't really want to reach back into that lion's den just to get hurt. We're both just trying to protect ourselves, so I guess we have a lot in common after all."

"I'm sorry," she whispers, reaching across the table to touch my hand. "You know I love you."

I send her a smile, forcing a look on my face that doesn't scream desperation and hopelessness, but I can't seem to shake this feeling. What I felt with Pax was something I hadn't felt with a guy before, and maybe it all happened too fast, and maybe I should take Everly's advice and start dating people my own age, but the idea of dating at all is out of the question. I need to get over this heartbreak first.

My week with Pax was a whirlwind, and it ended as fast as it started, making it hurt that much more.

13
PAX

By some miracle, I got to keep my job. My boss showed up that night so relieved that I wasn't dead that he didn't fire me or throw much of a fit about the fire. He pretty much let me in on the fact that he knew I was secretly sleeping in the garage, but since I never left a mess or made it too obvious, he didn't bother saying anything. I knew the space heater was a stupid thing to use in the shop in the first place.

After the fire, I got a call from Cullen, who not-so-nicely threatened that if I didn't take his girlfriend up on the offer of staying at their house, he would report it to the coach. It's not like I'd be punished for being without a home, but it would get messy. And even though I don't know much about Ayers, I know him enough to know he's been through shit too and probably hates pity as much as I do. If not more.

And it hasn't been bad. I'm never home anyway. I work late, study at the library until they close, and by the time I sneak into the house, it's dark and their bedroom is quiet. Thank God.

I haven't spoken to Thomas either. I sneak into his class, do my work, and sneak out. I'm too mortified by what I did to him that night to even look him in the eye. I can't take it back and I can't make it right, but I hope he at least knows I hate myself for it now. That was the cruelest I've ever been in my life. Not only did I blame him for the fire and for me *being gay*, but I literally blamed him for making me happy for a split second in time.

What the actual fuck?

And I knew my mistake almost immediately. I was just angry that night, letting my mouth run when I should have just kept it shut, let the whole thing pass, and worked through it all the next day. Because when I woke up the next morning, I regretted every last stupid thing I said.

Richards is talking to Hailey when I walk into English class. There's an empty spot next to him, so I quickly take the seat, but he doesn't greet me right away. He's been acting weird ever since the fight when he saw me with Thomas in the locker room.

Not bad, just weird.

He doesn't rip on me anymore. No more calling me ugly or cracking jokes about my face. None of the guys do, and it's driving me nuts. It's like they're walking on eggshells around me, and I just want everything to go back to normal. Be the same assholes they were before.

When Thomas walks into class, I notice he's

looking a little more disheveled than normal. His pants have wrinkles at the bottom, and his shirt is unbuttoned at the top. There are bags under his eyes, like he's not sleeping, and instead of greeting the class with that charismatic smile, he just walks in and finds me with his eyes. After giving me a quick, tense glance, he looks away and doesn't look at me again for the rest of the class.

The sooner this semester is over, the better.

This time after Thomas stares at me, I glance sideways, noticing Mason staring at me too.

Great. Just great.

As if I didn't already want to be invisible.

The rest of the day drifts by in a mindless blur, and at practice, I almost lose my mind when no one says shit to me after I blow the worst scrimmage in the history of rugby. In the locker room, I toss my bag harshly against the floor after my shower, turning around to find Mason standing by the door, staring at me.

"What?" I snap.

"Nothin." He shrugs as he moves to the sink and starts washing his hands. "You okay, man?" he asks without looking at me.

"I'm fine."

But he doesn't leave. He just stands there and continues to watch me, leaning against the bathroom counter.

"What the fuck, Richards? You got a problem?" I hate that my initial reaction is snapping at him, but he's freaking me out. My cheeks burn as I'm flushed with paranoia. I can just tell he's about to say something.

"So, Hailey and I started seeing each other," he replies, and I furrow my brow in confusion.

"Okay..."

"I think she liked you at first, but I didn't think you'd be mad about it."

"I'm not mad. It's fine, man." I toss the wet paper towel in the trash and pray this conversation is over. But he steps in front of me when I try to leave.

"I figured you were seeing Litchfield anyway."

The heat in my cheeks is rapidly replaced by ice in my veins as I stare unflinchingly at him. The words 'what the fuck' are on the tip of my tongue, but they don't come out. I just want to see what would happen if I didn't freak out and get all defensive like I usually do.

"You were, weren't you?" he asks again, and I read every inch of his facial expression for disdain or disgust, but there is none.

"It was nothing," I mutter, the lie tasting vile on my tongue.

"I'm sorry for what those assholes said on the day of the fight. Ignorant fucking pricks."

"It's fine," I grunt.

"No, it's not."

He's right. It's not fine, but my brain is caught in a whirlwind after being ambushed by this conversation and coming out without even meaning to. And how much he doesn't seem to care.

"The team's got your back, you ugly fuck," he says, clapping a hand on my shoulder.

And I laugh because thank fuck he can at least act like nothing's changed, and I'm not a fragile baby just because I also happen to be ugly and gay.

"Thanks, Richards," I say, shrugging away from his hold.

"So what happened with Litchfield? He's out of your league or something? He's too pretty for you."

"Fuck you, Mason." I laugh, knocking him into the wall. "I am *never* talking to you about anything ever."

"Come on!" he whines, following behind me out to the nearly empty parking lot. "You hooked up with a hot teacher. I need details. I don't care that he's a guy."

"Never happening," I call back to him, holding up a middle finger as I walk toward Aphrodite.

When I notice the lonely BMW sitting on the other side of the lot, I pause. I remember the first time I saw that car, him sitting in the driver's seat, and I know Mason's right. Thomas is out of my league, but if I was the kind of guy who could grow balls and apologize for being an idiot, I would absolutely ask for another chance. Too bad I'm not though.

14
THOMAS

"You've gotta be fucking kidding me."

I turn the key in the ignition again, but it does nothing. The dash is on, the gas tank is full, but there is absolutely nothing happening when I turn the key again. I swear this week couldn't get any worse.

Parked in the school parking lot, it's starting to get dark. I could call Everly, have her come pick me up and just leave my car here. In fact, I probably should just leave it here, light it on fire, let a family of rabid raccoons move into it. This stupid piece of junk has only brought me bad luck.

Well, technically it brought me Pax, which I thought was a good thing, but after that disaster at the shop, I'm counting it as bad luck now because I have literally never been so miserable after a relationship. Even though Nico hasn't called me once, I don't seem to care. But seeing Pax every day...sucks.

I decide to leave the car problems for tomorrow

and pull up the Uber app on my phone. I have big plans of going home, alone, getting drunk and trying to forget everything that happened. My finger hovers over the Request Pickup button.

What if I just called him? What if I used the car as an excuse to see him again, outside of the classroom? If I were to call roadside assistance, that's who they would send out, right? So I'm just cutting out the middleman.

Without thinking about it anymore, I pull up his number and hit dial. While it rings, I blame Everly for programming his number into my phone, knowing full well she was tempting fate.

It rings twice before his deep voice breaks the silence. "Hello?"

"My car won't start," I say, starting with the concrete details, so I don't get stuck stammering on about feelings and regret.

"Oh, really?"

"I don't know if you're even working tonight, but I figured I'd call you first. See if you can tow it again."

"Hmm..." He hums across the line. "I'm not working tonight, but I can come look at it. I'll be there in fifteen minutes."

"Thanks," I reply, trying to ignore the subtle rush of excitement I feel at knowing he's coming here now. "I'm in the school parking lot," I add, just before the line goes dead.

Fifteen minutes later, the familiar black and silver muscle car loudly announces his approach, and

I look up to see him pulling into the spot next to mine.

The first thing I notice is that he looks good. I mean, he always looks good, but Pax is usually hiding in long sleeves and oversized sweatshirts. He cut his hair, which is now no longer hanging in his face. It's cropped short, faded at the sides and long on top. It shows off more of his scars this way, which I find odd for him since he's always so insistent on hiding them.

He has on a tight short-sleeve black polo shirt and jeans. My eyes are caught staring at him for a moment, wondering if he got all dressed-up just to see me. And I don't know how I feel about that. Well, I know I feel good about it, but I know that I shouldn't. I wish I didn't care. I wish Pax didn't have this effect on me and I wasn't so hung up on this one guy—but I am.

"Hey," he mumbles after getting out and staring at me with those broad arms crossed over his chest. I'm immediately taken back to that night on the floor of the garage, how hot he was beneath me, and a spark of heat travels down my spine.

Nope. I need to stop thinking about that.

"It won't start," I reply.

He doesn't respond, but I can tell by the furrow in his brow that he wants to say something.

"How are you?" he asks.

Taking a deep breath, I mentally prepare myself for a conversation that could either be great or terrible and what's even worse is that I don't know which way I want this to go.

So, I just shrug in response.

"Yeah, me too."

We're standing together in silence before I finally move away from the open door of my car. Gesturing toward the driver's seat, I say, "Want to pop the hood? You already know I don't know how."

He laughs, a deep, sexy chuckle that just makes everything worse. Why did I call him? This was stupid. I'm going to end up heartbroken again.

"I'm sorry for being an asshole," he says, without moving toward my car.

"It's fine, Pax. Water under the bridge."

He steps forward so there's only a couple feet between us now. My heart rate starts to pick up speed.

"No, it's not fine. I like you a lot, and I do this stupid thing where I sabotage anything good in my life, and I never fucking apologize, but you already know what a stubborn idiot I am. I think...that's why we worked so well."

He takes another step closer, and I can smell his cologne. It's intoxicating.

"Pax," I say, putting up a hand, but he closes the distance with another step, so my hand lands against his chest, and I don't move it away.

"I came out to my team," he says in the next breath, and my eyes snap up to his face.

"You did?"

"I don't know what I was so worried about. Most of them knew, and they all have my back. Literally nothing bad happened after I opened up, so I don't know why I was so worried."

"I'm happy for you," I say softly. My hand is still resting against his hard chest—I feel his rapid heartbeat beneath my fingers. He puts his hand over mine and takes another step closer, so we're standing toe-to-toe.

His face is just inches from mine.

"See? You don't need me after all," I whisper, keeping my gaze away from his. I know once we look into each other's eyes, it's over for me, and I'm not quite ready to let my guard down.

But then his fingers touch the spot just under my chin and he tilts my head up until I'm staring at him. "I don't. But I still want you."

There's no hope for me at this point. I realize just how far he's come since the first time. At that point, he was so defensive that he acted so damn aggressive; I could have never gotten anything like this out of him.

Now, as we gaze into each other's eyes, I know he's leaving it up to me to make the move this time, so I grab him by the back of the neck and drag his lips toward mine. As we crash into one another, he wraps his arms around me, hugging me so tight I can barely breathe. A gravelly moan hums through his chest, and my dick responds. He's already hard, his thick erection pressed against my belly.

The kiss is hungry and erratic, his teeth biting my bottom lip as I lick my way into his mouth. This is reckless of me, I know it, but I am addicted to him. His passion and intensity is like nothing I've had before, and I just want more. Is there a chance he'll shut down on me again, push me away and break my heart...maybe. Will it be worth it? Fuck yes.

The parking lot is dark now, and there's not a soul around as he backs me up against my car and grinds his hips against me in a slow but strong rhythm that makes my knees weak.

"I need you naked. Right. Now," he groans against my lips.

"The feeling is mutual," I reply, reaching behind me for the handle to the back seat.

"There's no way we're both fitting in there," he says, trailing his lips down the side of my neck.

"You got a better idea?"

Pulling away, he looks around as if he's actually searching for a place suitable for two men to discreetly fuck. Naturally, there's nothing. And the idea of driving all the way back to my house sounds like torture. I want him now, in the midst of all of this heat and excitement.

"Back seat it is," he replies in a stifled groan. His hands are still tightly wound around my waist, and as one lowers to my thigh, lifting my leg so he can grind against me even deeper, I let out a moan, considering letting him fuck me right here. It would be worth a night in jail, easily.

When I finally yank open the door to the backseat, he climbs in first, shuffling with his zipper and pulling out his hard cock before I even climb in behind him.

Then, he tears off his black shirt and throws it up front.

"Get on my lap," he commands, yanking my body until I'm straddling him. He comes in for a hungry kiss again.

I wrap my hands around his cock and stroke him, loving the strangled sounds he makes as I do. It makes his kiss even harsher, like he's starving for my mouth. While I work him with my hand, he undoes my pants and shimmies them down enough to pull out my cock.

It's pretty clear we won't be having sex in here. I'm already hitting the top of the car as it is and there's not a single position we could manipulate our bodies into in this cramped space, but with my body pressed hard against his and our shafts aligned so he can fit both in his giant hand, stroking them together, I'm not complaining.

The windows are already fogged up. I'm pressed tightly around him, and he starts to pick up speed with his hand, stroking us both together. The heat of his cock against mine is so fucking delicious, I couldn't keep my hips still if I tried. My body thrusts in the same cadence as his, our lips locked and our chests heaving in unison.

"I'm going to come," I groan.

"Me too," he replies in more of a grunt than words.

Our breathing changes as the heads of our cocks swell together. He unloads first, and I watch his face as his orgasm unravels him. His lips fall open, and his eyes squeeze shut. His inhales become choppy and stifled as the cum shoots across his chest, landing across his scarred pecs and collarbone.

"Fuck," I gasp, because watching him come was enough to send me over the edge, and I lose myself in the current as well. I love seeing my cum land in the puddles of his.

My body is spent, exhausted and satisfied as I slump against him. My head rests against his shoulder and his hands move in slow strokes across my back.

The car grows quiet as our breathing regulates, and I feel all of the thoughts I was pushing aside during our kiss float to the surface.

"You're going to break my heart, aren't you?" I mumble against his bare shoulder.

"I don't want to," he replies, pressing his lips to my head.

Pulling my head off of him, I grab a stack of napkins in the center console and get to work cleaning up the mess we made. I take slow, easy strokes across his body. I love looking at him, seeing the strength in each of his scars.

He grabs my chin and forces me to look at him. "Thomas, I was serious when I said I really like you. I like the way I feel *about myself* when I'm around you. I mean...look at me," he says, gesturing to his bare chest. "Guys are not busting down my door and they never will."

My brow furrows as I stare at him. And I understand what he's afraid of. Being vulnerable, giving someone else the opportunity to hurt you, is fucking scary as it is. So I can only imagine how being hurt so badly, by the one person who is supposed to comfort and nurture you, set Pax up for a life of fear and loneliness.

"I don't understand why you think these make you look ugly." I run my fingers over them again. "Pax, where you got them is ugly, but the fact that you're still here and you have these scars means you're fucking strong. You're a fighter, and that's not ugly. I think it's hot as hell."

Bending down, I press my lips to his collarbone, where an especially gruesome scar distorts the shape of the sharp bone underneath. His arms wind around my back and he squeezes me closer.

We sit there like that for a while before finally climbing out of the car. The fresh air feels like heaven to my lungs after sitting in that stifling space for so long, but once we get out, I remember my stupid fucking car won't start.

"I guess I should be thanking this stupid thing," I say, pointing to the hood. "But I still hate it. How much is this repair going to cost me?"

"Oh yeah," Pax replies, rubbing the back of his neck. Then he drops down to the ground, crawling under my car. I see a small flashlight beam as he tinkers around with something.

"What are you doing?" I call.

"Reconnecting your starter."

It only takes him a moment. I watch in confusion

as he scoots out, jumping up to wipe the dirt off his pants. "Go ahead, try it."

Getting in the driver's seat, I put the key in the ignition and turn. Just like that, the car starts right up. "Well, that was an easy fix. How the hell did my starter get disconnected?"

Leaning over me with his arm braced against the top of my car, he grimaces. "I disconnected it."

My face falls. "You what?"

"Listen, I'm sorry. I'm just not good at this dating stuff and I didn't know how else to get you to talk to me."

"You pick up the phone, Pax." I'm literally in shock, but with the way he's towering over me with those intense eyes and full lips and that mischievous smile, I couldn't even try to be mad. "I expect a real apology when we get to my place. Get in your car. Let's go."

Before jogging over to his own car to follow me back to my house, he leans down and plants a strong kiss against my lips. "Yes, Mr. Litchfield."

I swear this guy is going to break my heart, and I'm going to love every second.

The End

EPILOGUE
PAX

Four years later

"Get em' Pax!" I hear my man's voice from the chorus of cheers in the crowd as I rush down the pitch, slamming into the players on the other team. When the Forward tumbles, losing control of the ball, Thomas howls with the delight. "That's my man!"

I laugh as the play continues, sneaking a glimpse of him in the bleachers, fully decked out in his team shirt, looking hot as fuck in those dark blue jeans.

This isn't by any means an important game or even the big leagues of rugby. It's a local team that meets up in city parks on weekends. The crowd is made up of the players' families, kids, spouses and all. And a few female spectators who show up specifically for my best friend. Real *spectators*.

Mason winks at the girls as we jog together toward the sidelines.

I roll my eyes with a chuckle as I punch him in the shoulder. "Your fan club is more embarrassing than mine."

"Who's embarrassed?" he replies. "Looks like we're both getting laid this afternoon."

When I glance over at the two girls making flirty eyes at Mason, I try my best not to grimace. "Both of them?"

He shrugs. "Maybe."

Cullen darts between us, smacking us both hard on the back of the heads. "Get your heads in the game."

I throw my hands up in response. And here I thought I just played defense and stopped the other team from scoring.

By the end of the game, I'm a sweaty stinky mess. But it doesn't stop my boyfriend from pulling me in for a kiss in the bleachers.

"Good game," he mutters after pulling his mouth from mine.

"Thanks, babe," I reply, brushing his hair out of his eyes.

"You guys wanna grab some lunch?" Everly asks as Cullen slings a sweaty arm over her shoulder. She doesn't seem to care much either.

When Thomas and I glance at each other, I know what he's thinking.

"Umm...maybe next time, babe."

"Oh, right," she says as realization clicks.

"What did I miss?" Cullen asks.

"It's their anniversary," she adds with a coy smile.

"Oh damn. Well, get out of here. What the fuck are you waiting for?" Cullen replies, shoving me on the shoulder.

Thomas rolls his eyes before giving Everly a quick hug and waving goodbye to Cullen. Then he links his fingers with mine and we walk out to the parking lot.

Aphrodite is there waiting for us. I toss my bag in the trunk and slam the trunk, staring for a moment at my hot as fuck boyfriend standing near the passenger seat. He locks eyes with me for a moment, shooting me a small smile before pulling open the door and climbing in.

After I graduated from college, I got a promotion at the shop, and after a year working as a manager. With my new skills in business, I was able to increase our profits and clientele, making Olympus one of the best rated and busiest shops in Florence.

The only downside to this is that it's currently too busy in the shop today to take my boyfriend to the office and fuck him over my desk like I did for the first time four years ago.

Instead, I pull his hand to my lips and kiss his knuckles before yanking him closer to me and taking his mouth in passionate kiss. He groans as I sweep my tongue against his, and I feel this growing more heated by the second.

If I had known being in a relationship would mean having so much sex, I would have started dating a lot earlier than I had. But I remember the stubborn asshole I was when we met. Since meeting Thomas and having him to help me fully come out and experience life as a confident gay man, it's been like being born again.

I let him take me out to night clubs and gay clubs... and other kinds of clubs. He loves that. Being fucked in public. Letting me blow him in front of others, as if he wants to show me off.

I'll never want another man as long as I live. Thomas is perfect in every way, and yet he treats me like I'm the God. Like my scars aren't flaws, but beauty marks.

He wants everyone in the world to know I'm his.

And I want that too. Hence the box burning a hole in my pocket and my tightly wound nerves.

"Let's go home and finish this," he mumbles against my lips.

"Okay," I reply, reluctantly pulling away.

It's beautiful out for September, so we roll the windows down, put on the chill acoustic music Thomas loves and we drive through town like that, our hands still entertained on the seat between us.

"I love you," I say to him when we pull into the driveway.

"I love you too, babe," he replies, leaning over to kiss me again.

After a quick peck, we climb out of the car and rush into the house. Once we get there, we head straight for the shower. Our dicks are already hard as we shed our clothes and climb into together.

When he tries to kiss me again, I wrap my hand around his throat and smile. "Turn around," I growl, my lips against his. He licks his lips and does as I say.

My hand is still around his neck as his back is pressed to mine. He plants his hands on the wall and lets out a deep, husky groan that I feel through my grip on his throat when I reach down and stroke his dick.

"What if I had never walked into the office that day?" I mutter into his ear. "What if I had never fucked you over that desk?"

"We'd still be a couple of miserable pricks," he replies.

Then I run my cock between his cheeks, grinding myself against him.

"Fuck me, Pax," he rasps.

Just like the day we met, I lube up my cock with the stuff we keep in the shower, this time skipping the condom, one of my favorite things about being in a relationship. Then, I fuck him quick and dirty until the only sound in the room is our grunting and our bodies slapping together.

His hands are still pressed against the tile as he rocks his hips back on my cock, and just the thought of filling him up takes me to the climax of my pleasure.

"Oh fuck..." I grunt loudly when I come.

"Yes, babe," he replies, "I'm coming too."

I watch him shoot his load all over the shower wall, and then I pull him flat against my body, holding him there as we catch our breath.

"I'd like to take you to bed and do that again. But I want to take my time." My lips are against his ear as he reaches up to pull my face closer.

"Sounds perfect."

I slip my cock out of him, but other than that, we don't move as the water washes over us. I just hold him in my arms, loving the way he feels here. Wishing it could be this way forever.

With that thought, I pull my head off his shoulder and decide this is the moment.

"Thomas," I whisper.

"Yes, babe?"

"Will you marry me?"

He tenses, his hands over mine. Then he spins and stares up at me. I'm trying to read his expression for anger or fear or hesitation, ready for him to say no.

Instead he grabs my face and smiles. "Of course, I will."

My heart practically beats its way out of my chest and my face spreads with a big smile. "Yes?"

"Yes, Pax. I never thought I'd want to be with someone forever. Before I met you, I couldn't imagine a relationship like this, but you are the best thing that's ever happened to me. I would marry you in a fucking heartbeat."

Tears prick my eyes as I gather him up in a tight hug, practically lifting him off the floor. I feel his chest shudder as I hold him, and I can't tell if he's laughing or crying or both. But I've honestly never been happier.

I thought love would never truly happen for me. After such a rough start in life, I thought that being alone would be the best I'd get. I never thought I deserved a love like this, but this man proved me wrong.

————

Read Cullen and Everly's story in Burn for Me: geni.us/BurnForMe

ACKNOWLEDGMENTS

I loved writing Thomas and Pax so much. I really appreciate everyone who helped me bring their story to life.

Thank you to these amazing people:

Adrian, for always being such a loyal beta reader. I appreciate you so much.

Tits, for encouraging me and being the biggest cheerleader.

Jose, for the love and support of this series. Yes... there will be more. I don't know...maybe there's a new coach? ;)

My editor, Rebecca.

My proofreader, Rumi Khan.

My publicist and friend, Amanda Anderson.

My assistant, Lori.

My amazing ARC and street team for supporting me always.

And to everyone who has ever felt as if being alone was safer than being vulnerable enough to fall in love.

Fall anyway.

ALSO BY SARA CATE

Bully romance

Burn for Me

Boy of Fire & Ash

ABOUT SARA CATE

Sara Cate writes forbidden romance with lots of angst, a little age gap, and heaps of steam. Living in Arizona with her husband and kids, Sara spends most of her time reading, writing, or baking.

You can find more information about her at
www.saracatebooks.com

Made in the USA
Las Vegas, NV
11 December 2022

61820474R00083